Peggy of the Cove
Secrets

Ivan Fraser

Library and Archives Canada Cataloguing in Publication

Ivan Fraser, 1945-
Peggy of the Cove: Secrets / Ivan Fraser
ISBN 978-0-9736872-7-9 Hardback

Peggy of the Cove: Secrets / Ivan Fraser
ISBN 978-0-9736872-6-2 Paperback

I. Title. II. Title: Secrets

PS8611.R38P444 2008   jC813'.6   C2008-900616-X

Ivan Fraser (Publisher)
Cathleen MacDonald – Motion Picture Enterprises Inc. – Story Editor

Ivan Fraser Studio
Peggy of the Cove® and Peggy of Peggy's Cove®
10235/6 Peggy's Cove Road
Glen Margaret, NS B3Z 3J1
902 823-2083   1 888 524-2252   Fax 902 823-2083
www.peggyofthecove.com ivan@peggyofthecove.com

Cover Design – Ivan Fraser
Cover Painting of Peggy – David Preston Smith
Dreamcatcher on the cover, made by Lynn Henry.

Printed and Bound in Canada by Friesens,
Altona, Manitoba, Canada R0G 0B0

Dedication

This book is dedicated to my four wonderful children.

Jay, the oldest, holds a degree in Business, but his friends encouraged him to join them in Korea, teaching English. He's been there over ten years, loving it, and the people. He just received his Black Belt in Taekwondo, and is working on his MA in English. May your teaching gift expand outside the borders of instruction in language.

Bethanne, my only daughter, began her picture-framing career at the tender age of six, and has worked her way to the top. She now manages the family business. Developing a natural talent, she has excelled in photographic and artistic skills. She is married to Shawn, and they have two wonderful little boys, Justin and Colton. May your artist dreams expand far beyond your highest expectations.

Ryan is studying Outdoor Pursuits at CUC in Alberta. He worked a year after graduating from high school. He has taken two trips to Belize, helping to improve the facilities at an orphanage. Ryan also collects knives, and loves scuba diving. May you guide many adventurers through the beauties of nature in our amazing wilderness.

Brandon, the youngest, is exceptionally talented in drawing portraits and animals. He created the coloring book, *Peggy's Favourite Coloring Critters*. He is currently studying psychology at MSVU, in Halifax. He has made the Honors list, and is aiming for his Masters. May you bring hope and peace to the many troubled souls you will meet.

Ivan Fraser

Contents

Prologue

As the young girl thrashed about in the cold roaring sea, praying for deliverance, a huge wave washed her high onto the cold smooth rocks where she lay exhausted. Before the backwash from another merciless wave sucked her back into the ocean, a spark of hope lifted her spirits. She felt strong arms gently cradle her limp body and rush her to safety. A thick blanket was thrown around her chilled bones, blocking the fierce winds that had intensified her misery. Shivering with fear and cold, she buried her face against the man's warm neck. It felt like a flaming fire against her freezing, blue skin. Her heart raced, knowing she was safe, rescued by this courageous man. The girl's tears of fear turned to joy, as they flowed freely, soaking the stranger's collar.

Through blurry eyes, pieces of wreckage were all that she could see of the ship while crying for her Mama and Papa. At that moment she couldn't picture them in her mind. Terror filled her heart, realizing she couldn't remember her past.

The shouting from the crowd of onlookers confused the young girl as the man carrying her raced to the nearest home. He charged through the door, where a blast of warm air greeted them. A young man stoked the stove. The young girl was so cold she wanted to crawl in. Ladies ushered the man carrying her to a cozy lamp-lit bedroom. He placed her on a soft bed and left.

Confusion raced through the little girl's mind as the strangers commented:

"Look at the poor thing."

"She's turned blue. It's a wonder she survived."

"Will she live?"

"Get her out of those wet clothes."

A gentle woman they called Mary quickly dried her, dressed her in a warm flannel nightgown, and wrapped her in wool blankets before carrying her to the kitchen. Sitting beside the blazing hot stove, Mary held the young girl close to warm her chilled body, and stroked her long golden hair in hopes of calming the fear revealed in her deep blue eyes.

The child stared with uncertainty and hid her face when they asked for her name and where she was from. Mary, the only one who seemed to understand, asked the ladies to leave her be. "I can't remember who I am or who my Mama is," she whispered in Mary's ear, sobbing while clutching tightly to the one who brought comfort.

"It's alright, you're safe now. We'll take good care of you," assured Mary in a soft voice and placed her warm hand against the girl's chin to relax her chattering teeth. The girl wished the hand of love was her Mama's.

Another lady fed her a bowl of hot soup while Mary continued her cuddling. Heat from the potbelly stove slowly penetrated to her very bones, causing her to fall into a deep sleep from exhaustion.

She woke alone, in a strange bed in a strange land. Fear seized her thoughts as she rolled face down onto the pillow in a cry of anguish. Mary entered. They embraced each other for a long time in silence before Mary gently suggested they talk. The girl's heart swelled when Mary invited her to join their family and asked if she liked the name Peggy.

Mary took Peggy to her home, where she soon met her three sons; James, Peter, and Joe. Boys, she pondered, but couldn't remember ever having brothers. Before sorting which name belonged to each face, a big man strolled through the door. Mary introduced him as her husband, John. Peggy stood aghast. Before her stood the strong, brave man who had rescued her. She remained speechless. He walked over, kneeled down, looked deep into her eyes, and hugged her. "You saved my life," she breathed.

Mary busied herself with dinner to regain her composure. The boys washed up and rearranged the table, placing a setting where their little sister Elizabeth formerly sat. "This will be your place at the table," smiled John.

As time moved on, Peggy adjusted well to her new life in the Cove, thankful for the good fortune of being taken in by such a loving family. However, that didn't stop the gnawing pain of her amnesia. Over the next few years, people, places, and things sparked familiarities of her past. The compelling desire to discover her identity was set in motion.

Chapter 1
Peggy's Calamities

It was the loud rapping that stirred Peggy from her sleep. A frantic bombardment of knocks, similar to those made by the ship's timbers cracking from the raging sea, caused Peggy to shudder.

When she woke enough to move, she held in her hands a damp clump of what felt like seaweed ripping away from the rocks. When she grabbed for another clump, her eyes snapped open to see she was clutching her quilt.

Peggy was drenched in sweat and blinked to clear her eyes. She could see a beam of sunlight glistening off the brass bed-frame. Beyond the bed on the side-table sat the chipped enamel washbasin and a ceramic jug.

Rap, rap, rap!

She sat bolt upright and turned toward the sound. There, flapping his wings and pounding his beak against the windowpane, was her seagull.

"Hector!"

Hector was interested in only one thing. He cocked his head from one direction to another with his beady eyes letting Peggy understand in no uncertain terms that he wanted to be fed.

Trying to calm her jangled nerves she jumped out of bed, eager to forget her dreaded nightmare, which reminded her of that appalling shipwreck. Quickly she changed into dry clothes and filled the washbasin. *Perhaps a good wash will clear my head,* she thought, but the sensation of cold water sent shivers down her spine. She grabbed the towel, vigorously drying her face and hair. It took several minutes before her trembling subsided. While brushing the tangles out of her hair, the delicious aroma of breakfast brought more pleasant thoughts. Just when her nerves were calming, another loud session of rapping drove her over the edge. Approaching the window, she gave the sharp warning, "Hector! That's enough! I'm eating first and if that isn't good enough, you'll just have to find your own breakfast."

With that, she left the room while Hector protested even louder.

Arriving downstairs, Peggy found John and Mary seated at the table with their two youngest sons, Peter and Joe. As Peggy made her entrance, Peter looked up and exclaimed, "What happened to you? It looks like you just kissed the cod!"

Bewildered, Peggy glared. Mary intervened before another rude remark flew back, "Peter! You shouldn't be so abrupt. What's gotten into you this morning?"

"Ma! I was only kidding and thinking about the race."

"Mary, you know Peter meant no harm," agreed John. "He's restless about the race."

"What race?" asked Peggy, although her distant gaze revealed she had more concerns than any old race.

"The boat race," announced Joe, excitedly. "Steven stopped by this morning. The boys made plans last night after we left the wharf. There's a prize for the winners, and all the losers have to kiss a cod."

"Ugh! Disgusting!" blurted Peggy, "You'd have to be insane to do a barbaric thing like that."

"Well, we don't plan on losing and the winners will be treated like kings all day long."

"Can you imagine kissing a cold, slimy cod? I wouldn't do that for the whole world! The race sounds like fun, except I suppose you know who will be there to ruin everything."

"You mean Billy?" responded Peter.

"Of course! Who else?"

"Now, Peggy, I know you don't like Billy, but be kind. He's never done you any harm," reminded Mary.

"Not yet, but he still thinks I was the one who put that sea urchin in his rubber boot. Last week he was limping until he saw me. Then he pretended his toes weren't swollen and sore, but I could see the pain in his face. He promised, 'Your day is coming.' Who knows when he'll pull one of his stupid pranks to get even? I wouldn't trust him as far as I could throw him."

"He saw you down at the wharf just before he put his boots on. If it wasn't you, who was it?" chuckled Joe.

"Never mind. I'm not telling, but it wasn't me."

"Just remember, be nice. That's all I'm asking," warned Mary.

Peggy didn't answer.

Thoughts of the race brightened her outlook for the day. Before long, she was thinking only of the fun that lay ahead and she forgot all about her horrible nightmare. "I'm off to the wharf," she announced to Mary after finishing her chores.

"Have a good day!" replied Mary with a little concern.

"I intend to."

On her way out the door, Peggy noticed her stilts resting against the house and impulsively grabbed them. She had asked John to cut long poles for her stilts and wanted the pieces where her foot stood to be at least two feet above the ground. Then she'd be able to take giant steps. Practicing on her way to the wharf would be another opportunity to become a better stilt walker than that Billy. Did I have stilts before? she wondered.

After hopping on and beginning her walk, a big smile spread across her face. Janet and her Pa were approaching. John had mentioned that Mr. Fraser planned to bring meat in exchange for fish, but didn't say when. "Hello Janet, and you too, Mr. Fraser. You're just in time for the big race."

"And hello to you, young lady," greeted Mr. Fraser.

"What race?" asked Janet.

"I'll tell you all about it on our way to the wharf. Come on, let's get down there before we miss all the fun!"

Janet had to walk quickly to keep up with Peggy. In no time they arrived at the wharf. Peggy drew attention from everyone around, including her closest friend at the Cove, Sally. "Oh good. Here comes Peggy on her stilts, fellows. Which one of you is going to try to beat her?"

"Who cares about Peggy and her old stilts," scoffed Billy. I can beat her any day, but we have a race to win so you and your little friend just buzz off."

Rosa, Billy's sister, saw the change in his attitude as Peggy approached. She wished he wasn't so mean to her, and found herself in an awkward position between her Pa and Billy. They always complained about Peggy, while she knew her as a kind, loving friend. In fact, it was rather exciting that folks of the Cove called them twin sisters. Sometimes the girls switched roles, which totally confused the older folks. They weren't quite sure who they were talking to.

As Peggy made her grand appearance, comments like, "You show'em, Peggy," and "You boys've met your match, now," bellowed from the cheery men who were cleaning the last of their cod. Their enthusiasm only boosted her confidence.

"Watch this, everyone. I'm going to take the longest steps I've ever taken," announced Peggy.

That's what you think! smirked Billy while scheming to humiliate Peggy and bring her down. "We'll see how graceful and elegant you are when I'm finished with you," he sneered under his breath.

Peggy, focusing on the encouraging crowd to her right, paid no attention to her footing. At the perfect moment, crafty Billy slipped a cod skin directly into the path of her left stilt.

"Bull's eye!"

Horror flashed across Peggy's face the instant her stilt touched the cod skin. Inside, Billy exploded with laughter. He quickly covered his ear-to-ear grin with both hands.

"Yowee! Heeeelp!" screamed Peggy, losing control of all limbs; trying to prevent her legs from doing the splits. Like a bird tumbling from the sky with a broken wing, she flew, flailing uncontrollably, her body in one direction, her stilts in another.

Her loud 'Aaaahhhh!' faded into muffled babbles as her twisting body landed into a huge trough, full of slimy cod liver. Two dangling legs kicking over the edge and desperate hands clutching the trough were all that could be seen of the defeated Peggy. Kissing a cod would be an easy chore compared to this. Her eyes burned and she longed to escape the stinking, slimy grave that held her captive, when she felt four hands pull her out. Rosa grabbed one arm and Janet held the other. "Are you hurt?" asked Janet.

"I can't open my eyes, they're burning!"

"Here, wipe them with my handkerchief," offered Janet.

As quickly as Peggy wiped her eyes, the dripping mass flowing from her hair repeatedly covered them. The boys roared with laughter at the transformation of the confident, pretty young lady; now a greasy, putrid sea creature, covered with slime, miserable and wretched.

"Somebody, please get some water! Wash me off!" cried Peggy, with arms hanging, and her head bowed as goo slithered down her body.

"You asked for it," said Billy, who was the first to offer his services. He dumped a bucket of water directly on top of Peggy's head. Others quickly joined in, and doused her until she considered jumping into the Cove in spite of her fears. "Enough!" she yelled, but Billy wasn't giving up until he emptied his last bucket. With an uppercut motion, he drove the water directly into Peggy's face. It hit with such force that water shot up her nose, bringing on a session of snorting and coughing.

"Stop it! You heard her! Enough!" shouted Sally as she gave Billy a quick push. The force sent Billy staggering backwards. He almost fell overboard while tripping over his own feet.

"That was a big mistake," warned Michael. "Look out! Billy's coming after you!"

"I'm not scared of him," answered Sally as she stood boldly with her arms on her hips.

Billy's attempt to charge almost ended in a second disaster as he slipped on the wet boards. On his second attempt, Mr. Garrison stepped in front of Billy, "Are you fellows going to race or not?" he said sternly. "If you are, get with it. We'll have no more pushing!"

"Mr. Garrison's right, guys. Let's go," agreed Peter.

To save face, Billy pointed to Peggy and began laughing.

Peggy was never so humiliated in all her life. She gathered her courage and wiped her face with a rag that Janet managed to dig up. The boys split their sides with laughter until tears flowed. "Oh, Peggy, that was worth a fortune. Do it again! Do it again!" they chanted.

Billy wouldn't let up, "You should enter the race, Peggy. You couldn't possibly do any worse."

"I would if I were bigger, you bully! You always pick on someone smaller or weaker!" snapped Peggy.

"Is that so? Tell you what, Little Miss Know-It-All; I'll finish in half the time as you, or you can be the winner. And since we really don't want you around the rest of the day, the only thing you have to do when you lose is kiss the cod. How about it boys; we gonna let Peggy and Janet make fools of themselves?"

"That's taking an awful chance, Billy. Janet's no weakling. Too risky." one boy warned.

"What's the matter, are you babies a bunch of sissies? Look at Peggy's toothpick arms. There's barely enough muscle to lift an oar, let alone row," he scoffed. "Am I the only brave one amongst you chickens?"

Not wanting to look like sissies, they let Billy shame them against their better judgment. "If you insist. We just hope you're right."

"Right! Of course I'm right! So, missy, are you brave enough to take on the challenge?" dared Billy.

"Maybe I will. I'll think about it."

"Think about it, eh? I guess you're just a coward! I knew it."

"Coward! Who said I was a coward?"

"I did. You're still scared to go outside the cove by yourself in a boat. Don't tell me you're no coward, you scaredy cat!" taunted Billy.

Peggy was devastated. Billy was right. Her mind flashed back to that horrific nightmare as she looked out to sea. She shuddered just thinking about it. She wanted to run and hide, but wasn't about to let Billy shame her again.

"You just wait a minute. I'll be right back," Peggy assured him as she took Janet aside, but in her mind the battle continued.

Being accused of cowardice hit hard, and thoughts of the present challenge and past fears competed. Every time she looked toward the vast sea a sickening nausea churned her stomach. She trembled at the very thought. She remembered being tossed around in that roiling sea before being washed onto the rocks. Images flashed before her eyes. She remembered John carrying her from the rocks and Mary coming into the room when she woke from her sleep, terrified from the ordeal, and not knowing who she was.

At that moment, Hector squealed and squawked as he circled overhead. Peggy wished she could fly away with him and be as brave as he was. No doubt he was scolding the boys for taking advantage of her dilemma.

Hector sensed Billy overdid his washing act on Peggy and was out for revenge. Without warning, he dove straight for Billy and let go with a load of soupy droppings that splattered down the side of Billy's head and neck. Billy shook his fist at Hector, threatening to get even. The boys turned to hide their laughter; knowing Billy only got what he deserved.

Peggy was so busy wiping her eyes that she missed Hector's attack on Billy.

"Are you alright?" asked Janet, snapping Peggy back to the present ordeal.

"Right now I have to settle this issue with Billy. Do you think any of the boys, especially Billy, could be twice as fast as we could?"

"I'm pretty strong, but if we lose, ugh! I don't know if I could kiss that revolting cod!" pondered Janet. "What do you think?"

"I think if I don't put Billy in his place today, he'll never stop torturing me!" fumed Peggy. "If we back down now, it'd be worse than losing. We'll show them we're no cowards!"

"I'm game, if you are," agreed Janet.

Impatiently waiting for the girls to make up their minds, Billy started again, "What's the matter, gonna run home to Mary? I knew you'd be chicken!" he chided as he walked around squawking, waving his arms, and bobbing his head like a scared chicken. By the looks of some of the boys, it was obvious they thought Billy was crossing the line, but wouldn't dare say a word.

"That's not true, you big bully. Count us in. We'll wipe that smirk off your face when *you* kiss the cod!" retorted Peggy.

"You two will be the ones wiping your faces," laughed Billy, rubbing his hands together. "Here's the list of rules. You two go last since we already have the order we're gonna race in."

The two girls read the list:

1 Two per team.
2 Teams must be even.
3 Same boat used by each team.
4 Stay within the course.
5 Three seconds added for each buoy touched.
6 Fastest team wins and become kings for the day.
7 All losers kiss the cod and serve the winners.

Peggy read the list. Those final words, 'All losers kiss the cod,' resonated in her mind. She looked up and stared ahead at the cove. That's when she saw Mary at the cove's entrance, beckoning Peggy to join her.

Reluctantly, Peggy obeyed. As she, Janet, and Sally

approached, Mary gasped, "Peggy, what on earth happened to you? Look at the mess you're in! Oh, my dear, you reek like rotten fish! Go bathe and change this instant," insisted Mary.

"Please, Mary! Not now," Peggy pleaded. "Janet and I are in the race too."

"In the race? Surely you don't expect to win! What's happened to you since breakfast? You thought kissing a cod was disgusting!"

"It was that Billy. He called us cowards. We're going to show him a thing or two. Please! Don't make me change now. I'll do it after the race."

"I suppose. I hope you don't catch a death of a cold."

"Don't worry about me; I'll be fine. Thank you, Mary! We want to see how the race goes. This is the perfect spot to watch them turn around."

"Fine," agreed Mary, "but you sit downwind. Nobody wants to smell that odor."

They watched as each team took their turn. Now it was time for Peter and Joe. When they finished, Mr. Garrison shouted, "Seven minutes and forty-six seconds!"

Everyone shouted and cheered. Billy and Andy were the second last team; Peggy and Janet were getting nervous.

"Come on Andy, let's show them how to row. You take the seat closest to the bow, steer and keep in time with me. We'll be kings for the day!" Billy proudly announced as they pulled together.

Although their speed amazed the onlookers, Billy's uneven rowing pace made it difficult for Andy. He struggled to avoid clashing oars and warned Billy that his were coming too close to the buoys.

"You're the one steering," growled Billy, putting all the blame on Andy. "You better keep us from hitting them or else," he threatened.

Rounding the last marker and racing back, Andy couldn't keep silent "Careful! There's another buoy!"

"Don't tell me what to do. Just row."

"Oh, my dear! Did you girls see Billy touch that buoy with his oar?" asked Mary as she looked through her spyglasses.

"I thought it moved, but I couldn't tell for sure. How about you, Peggy?" asked Sally.

"Oh, it moved alright. I bet he won't tell the judge."

"Are you sure?" asked Janet. "Would he cheat?"

"Cheat?" exclaimed Peggy in a high voice, then realizing Mary wouldn't approve, calmly continued, "If he thought he'd get away with it, he might."

"Might?" shouted Sally, "There's no might about it. He hates losing. He'd do anything to win!"

"Now, girls," was all Mary had to say. By the tone of her voice, they knew it was time to change the subject.

"Come on girls, let's get over to the wharf. We're next," urged Peggy.

"Billy and Andy's time is seven minutes and forty-four seconds. The best yet!" announced Mr. Garrison. "That makes Billy and Andy the winners, unless Peggy and Janet can beat them."

Hearing the announcement brought a smirk to Billy's face that showed confidence and victory. He rolled with laughter and leaned over the starboard gunnel. While hidden from the onlookers, he secretly cracked the forward tholepin before tying the boat and climbing the ladder to join the crowd.

Peter and Joe were good sports, but disappointment was written all over their faces.

"Peggy and Janet, you're next," encouraged Mr. Garrison. Peggy was so nervous she flitted about like a butterfly so nobody would notice her trembling. She and Janet took their positions.

Mr. Garrison hollered, "Ready! Set! Go!"

"Pull, Janet," encouraged Peggy. "Row like your life depends on it!"

"That's exactly what I'm doing," laughed Janet.

They didn't say another word for some time. All their energy was in their rowing. Near the entrance to the Cove,

Peggy couldn't keep silent. "Look how fast we're going. I can see Billy kissing that cod now," she shouted.

"If we keep this up, we'll be the winners for sure," agreed Janet.

"That Billy is going to eat humble pie today. That'll teach him not to mess with us."

"We need to get ready to make the turn," warned Peggy. Glancing over her shoulder to get her bearings, she couldn't believe her eyes, "Mr. Manuel is sailing through the entrance of the Cove. We're going to collide," shouted Peggy.

"Pull over to the side, and let him go by," suggested Janet.

"No! There's not enough room," shouted Peggy as fear of capsizing seized her heart. "Quick Janet! Row for shore before we crash!"

"No! We'll lose."

"We'll sink if Mr. Manuel rams us!"

"Just go around him."

"Go ashore now!" ordered Peggy in a panic.

"Oh alright," groaned Janet, "but make it quick."

"I'll jump out and turn us around as soon as he goes by," assured Peggy as she leaped. Her jump forced the boat away from her. The exposed seaweed on the sloping rock made it impossible for Peggy to keep a solid footing. She began slipping toward the water and under the boat.

"Are you girls alright?" called Mr. Manuel as he passed by.

"I think so," said Janet. "We're in a race, and now we've lost a lot of time."

"Sorry about that. If I'da known I'da turned around and stayed out of your way."

"Thank you, Mr. Manuel, but it's too late now," replied Janet.

"Help! Janet!" shouted Peggy. "I'm going to drown," she yelled with a fearful cry while her arms waved frantically to maintain her balance. Fear of being swallowed by a watery grave haunted her since the shipwreck, now it was happening. Janet quickly pulled on the right oar. The bow swung just in time for Peggy to grab. By now she was knee deep in the water.

"Don't be silly. The worst that can happen is a little swim. That'll only help wash that stinky smell off. Hurry up and get in!" encouraged Janet.

"I'm trying!"

"Now hold the bow while I push the stern around so we can start back," instructed Janet.

As the boat swung, Peggy crawled aboard, and threw her oars in place. Desperate to make up for lost time, she pulled with such force, the tholepin that Billy had cracked, broke. "Great! Just great!" exclaimed Peggy in disgust. "Will anything else go wrong?"

"Hurry!" coaxed Janet as Peggy replaced the broken oarlock, "Maybe we can still win."

"I hope so," said Peggy as they took their positions. Pretend we are being attacked by a shark and we will be eaten if we don't row hard enough."

"Peggy! Where do you get your wild imagination?"

"I don't know, but wouldn't you row harder if you knew you were going to be a shark's lunch?"

"Yes! Yes! That's for sure, but I can't go any harder."

"And I can't stand the thought of facing that arrogant Billy if we lose. I can see him now."

Janet shouted, "Pull!"

"My arms feel like rubber. Now the wind is picking up. It's just not fair."

"Stop talking. Save your energy and row," Janet said. "We're almost there."

As they crossed the finish line, Mr. Garrison shouted, "Finished! Peggy and Janet are thirteen seconds late. Billy and Andy are the winners!"

"Finished is right," gasped Peggy who almost collapsed. She was devastated with their defeat, wishing she had stayed away, and far out of Billy's sight.

"Let's just sit here a minute, Janet. I need to catch my breath before facing that crowd. Look at that Billy, strutting around like a rooster in a flock of hens. It's disgusting!"

Billy entered the fish store and brought out a huge, slimy cod. "Alright, you can start kissin' now," he gloated, with a gleam in his eye. "Go in the same order as ya raced."

Poor Steven and Tim stepped forward. Steven leaned over, with his lips only an inch from the cod, hesitating.

"Come on, kiss that thing!" bellowed Billy.

Steven stepped back, and shook his head. Then gingerly, he leaned forward again to do his duty.

"Hold it! Hold it!" shouted Peggy, out of breath as she climbed the ladder. "We want to check on something, Mr. Garrison. Did Billy tell you his oar touched a buoy?"

The look on Billy's face was one of repulsion and anger. "Yer makin' that up. I'm the winner!"

"No, I'm not! Here comes Mary. She saw it, too. You ask her, Mr. Garrison."

The crowd stood wide-eyed, and felt the tension growing by the second.

"Yer just makin' that up 'cuz you're mad at me for slippin' that cod skin under yer stilt," hollered Billy, right into Peggy's face.

"You what? You did that to me?"

Everyone stood in disbelief. Nobody had noticed Billy's quick action; they had been focusing on Peggy's big smile.

Peggy just stood glaring at Billy, searching for words to tear him apart.

"My oar barely skimmed it, Mr. Garrison. I think it

was just the wind from my oar that moved the buoy. I really didn't touch it."

"I'm afraid a nick is a touch, Billy. Three seconds has to be added to your time. That makes Peter and Joe the winners by one second."

"No way; I'm the winner!" he shouted as he turned to stomp off.

What happened next shocked everyone. Peggy grabbed the cod with both hands and yelled, "Billy!"

Her shout stopped him in his tracks.

"What'dya want now, squirt?" snorted Billy, angrily, as he turned to face his opponent. Peggy's timing was perfect. It was now her turn for a bull's eye. Wham! That cold slimy cod smacked Billy directly across his face, almost knocking him off his feet.

"You forgot to kiss the cod, you loser! And another thing, don't you ever bother me again! Do you hear?" bellowed Peggy as she stood defiantly in front of him.

"You'll pay for this, little miss orphan. You just wait. I'll get you back. You don't even know your name. Huh! You're just a nobody!" he shouted while waving his head and turning up his nose.

"Don't you dare talk to my friend like that!" threatened Janet. "I bet she's a princess. You better learn your manners boy!"

"She's no princess. A pauper is more like it," retorted Billy.

"That's enough!" stepped in Mr. Garrison, trying to restore the fun they'd enjoyed earlier. "Come on, Billy, be a sport," he encouraged, while handing him a rag to wipe his face. "The race was all in fun."

Billy wouldn't change his mind. He stomped home, and didn't show his face the rest of the day.

"Peggy, what has gotten into you?" gasped Mary. "I've never seen you act like this before."

"Yeah Peggy, that was out of this world!" laughed Sally, with a twinkle in her eye while Janet stood with her hands covering her mouth and eyebrows raised.

Mr. Fraser and John arrived at the scene just in time to hear a number of boys chorus, "Peggy's gonna get a lickin'."

"What's all the commotion about?" asked John.

Mary quickly informed them of the events that caused the uproar.

"Now, now! Let's get back to the issue at hand," reminded Mr. Garrison. "It's time for you losers to take your position."

The jesting and laughter from the boisterous boys echoed throughout the Cove. Girls wrinkled up their faces as they imagined the horrible taste of that slimy fish. All the boys reluctantly did their duty. Janet and Peggy were next. Everyone watched eagerly as they took their positions.

Peggy stood tall, and stared at the crowd of boys in silence. Mary sensed something was brewing and grew fearful of what Peggy was contemplating. She wanted to intervene, but remained silent with bated breath.

"You boys are some cowards," she began.

"Oh no! John, do something," whispered Mary.

"Shhh! Just listen," he answered with a look of pride, and curiosity.

Peggy continued, "You call that little peck a kiss? Shame on you! Come on, Janet! Let's show them what a real kiss is!" And with that, Peggy grabbed the cod by the gills, pressed hard against its lips, and held on for what seemed an eternity.

The crowd remained hushed; then broke forth with yahooing, clapping, and cheering. "You show'em, Peggy!" yelled the fishermen. John, Mr. Fraser, and Sally clapped and hollered with the others. Even Mary got caught up in the jubilation.

Peggy instantly became the hero. She and Janet danced around, reveling in the respect they'd earned. However, as the excitement died down, Peggy was haunted by Billy's words, "You'll pay for this, little miss orphan."

Chapter 2
The Knottys

Barrister Oliver Knotty, of 125 Haggis Lane, Aberdeen, Scotland, was in a sweat; but it wasn't from the heat of the day. His huge gambling debt to Mr. Betts was due in two days or else. Oliver wouldn't be the first to disappear off the face of the earth if Mr. Betts wasn't paid on time. Oliver had assured Mr. Betts his debt would be paid long before the due date. But, without having paid one pence, Oliver was worried that Mr. Betts might have him followed, preventing his escape. Pacing the floor at his office, Oliver desperately searched for some miraculous way out before he was exterminated. A loud knock startled him. With a shaky hand he cautiously opened the door, relieved to see the person on the other side wasn't Mr. Betts. A messenger boy passed him a letter from Judge Sampson. Quickly ripping it open, Oliver was puzzled by what he found inside: the Judge requested his presence at his office at eleven o'clock sharp. Although eager to know what the Judge had in mind, Oliver was determined to appear calm as though he had no concerns, and was in no financial need.

Oliver was tall and had always been a bit on the thin side until recent years. He was filling out now that middle age had crept up on him.

Mr. Knotty left his office and walked briskly to his home, put on his finest suit, and set off to meet the Judge without delay. His erect posture and light step gave the appearance that he considered himself a man of great importance. As he strode down the main streets, his thoughts ran wild. Perhaps his long overdue promotion as a judge had arrived or some high government position awaited him. Whatever the case, he was a few minutes early, which would impress the Judge who detested tardiness. His daydreaming ended abruptly, when the scruffy character, Grub, caught up to him and shoved him into an alley, "Mr. Betts wants his money or else," threatened Grub.

Anyone who knew Mr. Betts also knew Grub, his henchman.

"Ah! Yes of course, Grub. Pass a message along to Mr. Betts, please. Tell him the money is on its way. I'll pay my debt in three," Oliver said in a shaky voice. He didn't clarify what the three meant, because he was stalling for time.

"Three? It's due in two," informed Grub in a gruff tone while grabbing Oliver by the throat and squeezing tight.

"Please let go, Grub, you're choking me," he wheezed with a quivering lip.

"Don't tell me what to do, you weasel. I'll let go when I'm ready."

"Yes, Grub. I was asking, not ordering. Please! Be reasonable. Surely we can work something out. What's it worth to give me a break?"

"Are you trying to bribe me?"

"No, of course not. I firmly believe a man should be rewarded for a job well done. If there's one thing about you, sir, it's that you do your job very well. Here, please take this as a token of my appreciation," insisted Mr. Knotty as he handed Grub a one-pound note and started to sneak away.

"Not so fast Barrister," warned Grub as he stuck out his foot and tripped Mr. Knotty. Oliver's desperate attempt to catch his balance, failed. He fell forward onto the dirt, tearing the right knee of his suit and soiling him from head to toe. The brim of his hat was bent; his chin and hands were scraped.

"Excuse me, Mr. Knotty. Make that two pounds, if you don't mind."

"Yes, by all means," he readily agreed, passing Grub another note.

"And this reward is to be our little secret. Right?" smiled Grub.

"Absolutely," agreed Mr. Knotty.

With that, they parted. Oliver, still shaking from fear and anger, straightened up the best he could, hastening to Judge Sampson's office. The clock struck two as he entered.

"I'm here at the request of Judge Sampson," announced Mr. Knotty to the secretary.

"Yes, the Judge is expecting you. Please go in." She looked puzzled at his distasteful appearance.

Judge Sampson welcomed him as they shook hands. "How good to see you, Mr. Knotty. It's been some time. My dear man, what happened to you?"

Oliver, not daring to reveal the truth, had an excuse prepared, "I was attacked on my way here!"

"Attacked? Can you identify the scoundrel?"

"I certainly can, your Honour."

"Well, contact the police so they can track that hoodlum down and put him behind bars where he belongs."

"It will be difficult to arrest a dog, sir. He appeared from nowhere, causing me to trip and fall. When I finally succeeded in fending him off, he limped away with his tail between his legs. I don't think he'll bother me again."

"Good for you, my man. And here I thought you were... well let's say, not the bravest when it came to fighting, if you remember our university days." The Judge then turned away so Mr. Knotty couldn't see his amused expression. Back when they were studying for their degree, Frank wanted to settle a quarrel over Hannah by fighting, but Oliver ran.

Not wishing to discuss the issue, Mr. Knotty changed the subject, "You wanted to see me?"

"Yes, of course, we'll soon get down to business. How have you and Mrs. Knotty been?"

"Very well, Judge. Couldn't be better, aside from this attack," he lied while thinking, *good to see me, my fat eye.* Frank detested the fact that Oliver always made higher marks and stole Hannah from under his nose. He also knew Frank's only interest was Hannah.

Oliver knew where to strike back, "And you, Judge, you never married?"

The Judge stiffened, turned a little red, and was about to make some profound statement, but caught his reaction just in time. "I'm too busy for family life, Mr. Knotty. Take a look around."

"Why of course, I understand," agreed Oliver, glancing at the fancy office, which had a large window, and much decorative oak woodwork that matched his desk.

"You like my office, I see. Try out my chair."

"Don't mind if I do," said Mr. Knotty as he sat in the large leather chair that offered more comfort than he could have imagined.

"Well... how does it feel?"

"Almost as comfortable as mine," smiled Mr. Knotty.

"I'm sure it is," came the Judge's reply in a deep powerful voice that sounded like it was echoing through a tunnel. To impress Mr. Knotty, he stood erect which made his stomach stick out even farther.

Oliver wanted to chide the Judge about overeating, his ridiculous oversized mustache and sideburns, and the thinning of the hair above both temples, but he refrained.

Meanwhile, the Judge knew Oliver was having financial difficulties, but not quite sure how serious they were. He was thinking about Mr. Knotty's earlier claim that his life "couldn't be better.' *What a laugh. You liar.*

"Do you still like to go on long trips, Mr. Knotty?"

"It depends on where and how long."

"Over three years ago, Frederick MacEve, his wife, Jane, and their only daughter, Hope, left Aberdeen, headed to the new land of Nova Scotia. They haven't been heard from since, nor has anyone seen their ship, *Little Miss Fortune.* The assumption was that everyone was lost...until now. Rumor has it that a young girl survived and she fits the description of Hope MacEve. I have been commissioned to investigate, and verify that this girl is Hope. There is an inheritance involved. Are you interested in going overseas to prove the girl's identity and bring her back, if indeed she is Hope?"

Mr. Knotty was ecstatic about the inheritance. Securing it would provide an opportunity to pay off his debt to Mr. Betts and revel in the lifestyle he and Hannah cherished. He hid his excitement from the Judge. His blood pressure rose, his heart pounded, and for a minute he paced around the office to calm his edgy nerves. He wanted to convince the Judge it was a heavy matter. He appeared to be in deep thought, debating whether or not he should accept the offer. Finally he replied, "Yes, I may be interested. When do you need a definite answer?"

"The sooner the better. You shouldn't wait too long or the return trip would put you in the hurricane season. I'm sure you'd like to avoid that, but then there's the question of Mrs. Knotty. Perhaps she wouldn't appreciate you being away for such a long period of time?"

That's what this is all about, that old buzzard, thought Oliver. His mind ran wild, convinced that Frank wanted to send him off so he could drop by occasionally to make sure Hannah was fine. He didn't trust Frank in the least and was worried about leaving Hannah alone. "Oh I'm sure Mrs. Knotty would love to come along. I'll talk it over with her and let you know this afternoon. How will that be?"

"Very well. I'll be out until about three. Stop by after that. Out of curiosity, what's your first impression of the assignment?"

"I rather like the adventure, but of course there are a number of issues to consider. I'll be back with a definite answer later today."

Mr. Knotty shook hands with the Judge and left.

"Hannah! Hannah!" shouted Oliver as he entered their home. "I have great news. How would you like to go on a holiday?"

"Oh, Oliver! You know I love holidays. Where are we going— My dear! Look at your finest suit. What have you been up to now?" she demanded.

He gave Hannah the same line he told Judge Sampson.

"I hope you don't get rabies!"

"No, of course I won't. The beast didn't break my skin. Now back to the holiday."

"Yes, I hope we're going to Paris?"

Oliver's heart sank, but he didn't want to show it. "No, you've been to Paris many times. We have the chance of a lifetime to go to Nova Scotia."

"Nova Scotia? Isn't that some forsaken barren land across the Atlantic? Why would we ever take a holiday there? No! I'd rather not. You'll have to do better than that."

"Well let me explain. You may change your mind after hearing my brilliant plan."

"I suppose I could at least hear you out. Tell me your brilliant plan. I've been waiting since our wedding day to see one of your schemes prosper."

"This is the best one yet. Now, here's what I have in mind," said Oliver as he explained his plan.

"Maybe this is the big one. It certainly has potential," agreed Hannah, who began scheming too, with a gleam in her eye. "Of course, you'll have to pamper me if I agree. I will be sacrificing the comforts of home on such a long trip."

"Don't I always take good care of you?"

"Not always, Oliver. Do you want me to remind you of the list of blunders that are stored in my mind?"

"Let's not spoil our trip. You start packing and I'll

make arrangements to leave on the first available ship. I believe we may find passage as early as tomorrow morning. You just be ready. I must go visit Judge Sampson at his office and give him our answer. I'll see about getting tickets as well."

"You mean Frank has arranged this?"

"Yes. Judge Sampson has appointed me above anyone else for once."

"How interesting. Dear old Frank. Say hello to him for me, would you?"

"I think not. He's still annoyed that I swept you from under his nose."

"Oh, Oliver, don't be silly. Send him my greetings."

Oliver headed out the door, relieved that Hannah agreed to his plan, but her amusement over Frank opened old wounds. The more he thought about it, the more annoyed he became until jealousy caused a gnawing pain in his stomach. He hastened on with a stern look and arms swinging. In his anxiety, he almost forgot to keep his eye out for Mr. Betts or his cronies. If he could just remain hidden for one more day, he'd elude Betts while finding the money to resolve his financial disaster.

As a front for his illegal dealings, Mr. Betts owned an importing and exporting business; he was a well-known figure along the docks and among the customs officials. Unfortunately, the customs office was near the ticket booth; Mr. Betts could show up anytime and spot Mr. Knotty purchasing tickets. Oliver would have a tough time explaining his situation, so he mingled among the crowd while checking for Mr. Betts or any of his men. Just as he was sure the coast was clear, Grub strolled through the door, followed by Mr. Betts.

Oliver recognized Mr. Betts' scrawny figure immediately and, even though he was weak in physical strength, his goons and influential power made Oliver tremble. His tiny glasses rested on the tip of his nose as usual and his hat almost covered his eyes, making it difficult for anyone to see where he was looking. At least his hat was forward, covering his gray hair. It was a known fact that whenever he pushed his hat back, it was a sure sign of trouble. Although Mr. Betts was past his prime in years, his conniving hadn't diminished. If anything he became worse with age.

Of all the miserable luck, thought Oliver as he slithered behind one person after another. Grub scouted the area as if on the lookout, while Mr. Betts walked into the customs office. Oliver panicked for a minute when he feared Grub had looked him straight in the eye. Crouching, he hid his face, but he must have looked rather suspicious. Finally, Grub turned toward the customs office and Oliver breathed easier. When Mr. Betts came out, they walked toward Oliver. With a quick turn, he bent over as if fixing his boot. Mr. Betts brushed against him, but was looking at Grub while instructing him to keep an eye out for Mr. Knotty.

"We wouldn't want him to slip away now, would we?" he said in an icy voice.

"Not on your life," agreed Grub, and they both laughed while going through the door.

Oliver's hands were still shaking at the ticket booth. His spirits rose when he discovered the *Flora M* was sailing the next morning for Nova Scotia. There was room for him and Hannah. With tickets in hand, he slipped off to give the Judge his answer.

As he stepped into the Judge's office, he greeted the secretary, "Is Judge Sampson back yet?"

"Yes, I'll tell him you're here," she replied as she knocked on the Judge's door.

"Come in, come in."

"Mr. Knotty is here to see you."

"Send him in."

As Oliver entered, Judge Sampson asked, "So what is your answer, my good fellow?"

Good fellow, my eye, thought Oliver. He knew that the

only time the Judge would put 'good' and 'Mr. Knotty' in the same sentence would be to call him 'good for nothing.' Oliver was anxious to see the disappointment on the Judge's face when he would discover Hannah was going to Nova Scotia. He smiled as he replied, "My answer is yes and so is Mrs. Knotty's. She wishes to come along with me. We'll leave first thing in the morning."

Oliver glowed as he watched Frank turn in disgust to hide his diving fist, "Mrs. Knotty wishes to go overseas?" he asked in a state of shock.

"Yes indeed," replied Mr. Knotty, all aglow. "We're going to make it our second honeymoon. Can't you just imagine how romantic it'll be? Me with Hannah all that time?"

The Judge was green with envy, but wasn't giving Mr. Knotty the satisfaction of knowing how jealous he really was. "That surprises me. Very well then, good luck Mr. Knotty. I'll be anxious to find out how you do," and he gave Oliver a hardy handshake that was more than comfortable, one that brought pain to Oliver. For a minute it became a contest as Oliver squeezed for all he was worth. Judge Sampson wanted to crush Oliver's hand, and could have, but realized he was only showing his jealousy.

"Here's a small framed portrait, a description of Hope MacEve, and the location of the girl we think is Hope. It will help you identify her. Is there anything else you need to know?"

"No, everything is in order," said Oliver, agitated, as he parted hastily. He was so anxious to get home, but he slithered through the back streets to avoid Mr. Betts.

Oliver convinced Hannah it was necessary to leave before daybreak because the ship might leave early. Of course his real reason was to avoid Mr. Betts and his gang.

The next day, Hannah was up very early to make herself presentable. Oliver was impatient and insisted on leaving. Reluctantly, Hannah hurried, and off they went.

Oliver, tense all the way to the dock, was relieved that

they finally arrived safely. He ushered Hannah aboard and went directly to their cabin until the ship was safely under way. It wasn't until they were past the lighthouse and out of the harbour that he relaxed. Matter of fact, he became so ecstatic that Hannah asked, "Oliver, why are you so happy all of a sudden?"

"Oh, I was tense about getting away. I expected some demanding business would prevent us from leaving. That hasn't happened. Now we are free with weeks to be alone. I believe you will be impressed with the plans I have in mind," he said in a devious tone, although he wasn't sure how he was going to manage to get his hands on the inheritance.

Chapter 3
Peggy's Big Awakening

During one of Janet's visits to Peggy's, she and Janet were heading outside to play when Mary, who wasn't having her best day, let out a sigh, "If I didn't know better, I'd say John had a sieve for a brain."

"Why is that?" smiled Peggy, trying to lighten Mary's burden.

"I asked him only minutes ago to take those old newspapers with him. They are piling up and cluttering my kitchen."

"Yes, but the minute you went upstairs, Mr. Garrison came to the door all out of breath. His old pig, Pinky, broke loose. He caught her, but she wouldn't budge so he tied her to the gate. He asked John to help push her home."

"Well! There you go. It doesn't pay to judge now does it?"

"We're going to the wharf. We'll take them," said Peggy.

"Thank you. Here, have a cookie. They're still warm."

"Thanks," said the girls as they raced down to the fish store with a cookie in one hand and the papers in the other. At the top of the steps to the loft, Janet stopped, "I just love it up here. It's so cozy and quiet."

"Yeah, and a great place to get away from Billy," agreed Peggy as she approached the box where John kept newspapers and magazines to start a fire.

"Wait! I want to see that magazine on top," said Janet

as she leaned over the box and blew to clear the dust. Since the edges of the box were fairly high, the dust backfired into her face, sending her into a sneezing frenzy. "Peggy—achoo—open my handbag—aaachoo—and find—aachoo—my handkerchief," she managed to ask between sneezes.

Peggy opened Janet's handbag and stood dazed by a strange object inside. "What's this thing?" she asked, forgetting all about the handkerchief.

"It's—achoo—a dreamcatcher."

"Dreamcatcher!" Peggy was spellbound.

"My handkerchief please!" asked Janet.

Peggy handed the handkerchief but was focused on the dreamcatcher. "I've seen one of these before, but I don't know where."

"Are you sure? When and where?"

Peggy didn't answer. Janet watched her fondle the dreamcatcher. Peggy was thousands of miles away. Seconds later she spoke, "I don't know."

"The Mi'kmaq people made that one. I wonder where you would have seen one like it? Were you ever up to Sarah's?"

"No. The Mi'kmaq? That doesn't help," said Peggy in a frustrated voice. "How am I ever going to remember where I've seen one of these?"

"Why don't you come home with me? We could visit Grandpa Knockwood and Sarah. Maybe talking to them will help you remember."

"I don't see how," sighed Peggy, who was beginning to weigh the consequences of finding her identity. On the positive side, she thought about the joys of meeting relatives who might be wealthy or even royalty. Would they be loving like Mary's family? It seemed impossible to find anyone better. Then the negative side brought fear. *Not likely. They're probably criminals or pirates who would force me to live on a pirate ship. Dealing with Billy would be a piece of cake compared to living on the ocean with storms and all that robbery and murder. After all, aside from Billy, life at the Cove is pretty good.*

"Well?" asked Janet.

No response.

"Hello! Is anybody home?" she questioned, staring directly into Peggy's eyes while tapping her on the shoulder.

"Oh! Yes... I was daydreaming. Janet! What if I have terrible relatives, and they make me their little slave?"

"What if you're a princess?"

"I could handle that with no problem. Can't you just see the look on Billy's face if I was?"

"That would be priceless," laughed Janet, "but if you don't start searching, you'll never see that look on his face. It's like treasure; you have to dig to find it. Why not at least come to my place, then you can decide if you want to visit Sarah and her Grandpa."

"Well...I guess I could do that."

"And you wouldn't have to look at Billy for days."

"That's the best reason yet."

"Come on, let's go ask Papa and Mary!" Janet coaxed, grabbing Peggy by the arm and racing down the steps.

As they were running toward the house, Peggy slowed her pace. She became silent again as her mind flashed back to the night of the dreadful shipwreck and Billy's dreaded words: 'little miss orphan.'

"I don't think I'll tell anyone about remembering the dreamcatcher. Will you keep it a secret, Janet?"

"A secret? Why? I thought you'd be telling everyone, especially Billy!"

"I don't know. I just want to wait. Besides, I don't know who I am yet."

"Well maybe you're about to find out."

"That's the scary part," hesitated Peggy before opening the door.

"Alright! I won't say a word, but this is going to be the adventure of your life. Now come on, let's go."

"Just remember, don't say a word."

"I promise," and Janet bolted through the door. "Papa, can Peggy come to our place for a while?"

Mr. Fraser didn't look up from the game of Chinese checkers he and John were playing, "I don't think so; you two might have too much fun, don't you agree, John?" he said while giving a little wink.

"I saw that wink, Papa. That means yes, Peggy. Oh thank you! Is that alright with you, Mary?"

"I don't see why not. It would give time for the dust to settle between Peggy and Billy."

"Yes, Yes!" shouted Janet. "When are we leaving Papa?"

"After dinner, when you help with the dishes and Peggy gets her things packed."

"Peggy, let's start packing right now," suggested Janet.

"You go upstairs Janet. Peggy, I'd like to see you for a minute," said Mary as she led Peggy outside.

"You can stay home if you don't want to go. I know something is bothering you."

"I want to go. Sometimes I just wish I knew who I was. Everyone else is so lucky."

It was one of those rare moments when Mary had a hard time holding back the tears. She embraced Peggy, and they held each other tight. "I better go pack," said Peggy. She hurried inside and up to her room.

Before they knew it, dinner was over, the dishes were washed, and they were on their way to Janet's.

Peggy was trying to look on the bright side as they made their way up the road. The Fraser Homestead was her favourite place to visit. Roaming the hills and paths through the woods always brought a sense of familiarity, and peace to her mind. But that day, roaming the hills wasn't on her mind. She was questioning whether or not to visit Sarah and her Grandpa, as Janet had suggested.

The next day, Peggy decided it was time to start her adventure. She agreed to the visit. Janet bubbled with enthusiasm while Peggy still had reservations, but knew her gnawing question had to be answered. She was more quiet than usual on their walk up the road. A surge of excitement raced though her mind at the possibility of discovering her past. When Peggy and Janet arrived at Wooden's River, Sarah's Grandpa was sitting on a nearby log working on another dreamcatcher. "Hello Janet," he greeted, "Who's your friend?"

Before having a chance to answer, a loud "Hi Janet," resounded from Sarah, as she hurried from the river with a pail of water. The right side of her dress was soaked and the wild flowers along the path were well watered as she ran to meet them.

"Hi Sarah. This is my friend Peggy. She's from the Cove."

"Are you Peggy of the Cove?" she asked with a big smile.

"Yes. How did you know?"

"Everyone knows about you. Did you know that you and I are something alike?"

"No. How can that be?"

"I lost my Mama and Papa too. Grandpa told me they fell asleep in icy waters when their canoe tipped over. I was too little to remember."

"I'm sorry," said Peggy.

"I know you understand," replied Sarah.

There was a quiet moment as both girls realized how the other felt about losing their parents. Grandpa broke the silence.

"It's a pleasure to meet you Peggy," smiled Grandpa as he reached to shake her hand.

"Thank you Grandpa," replied Peggy, but she was focused on Grandpa's dreamcatcher and couldn't take her eyes off it.

"You like my dreamcatcher?" he said cheerfully.

"I sure do and I know something about it, but I just can't remember! That's why we're here."

"Is that so? How can we help?"

"By telling me all about the dreamcatcher and what it does."

"Well, it's hung over your bed, or in the window to catch bad dreams before they reach you," he instructed.

"I sure could use one of those. I still get nightmares once in a while."

"Do you? Me too," exclaimed Sarah who began sharing her worst horrors. Peggy joined right in while Janet and Grandpa listened with interest. After exhausting every gory detail, Grandpa found a chance to slip in a word.

"I want you to have this. I hope it takes away your nightmares," and he handed Peggy the dreamcatcher he had just finished making.

"Really? Oh, thank you!" she exclaimed, barely able to contain her feelings. "Are you sure? You don't have to you know," Peggy replied, trying to be polite, but secretly hoping he would insist.

"I know, but I want you to have it. Besides, I have lots more. Now if you look on the back you'll see my initials, 'O-K.' That means Osprey Knockwood."

"Osprey, that's a different name," said Peggy.

"Isn't it funny?" replied Sarah. "When Grandpa was little, he always wanted to soar and fly like an Osprey, so his Mama called him Osprey. He liked it so much he still uses that name."

"That is funny," agreed Peggy.

"Is there anything else you'd like to know?" asked Grandpa.

"If you don't mind, Peggy wants to learn all about your people," said Janet.

"Oh you'll need to stay forever, right Grandpa?" said Sarah.

"I don't know about forever," replied Grandpa, "but a long time for sure."

"Just tell me as much as you can today," coaxed Peggy.

So Grandpa spent hours telling them all about the Mi'kmaq people. They walked up and down the river and around the lake until it was time to leave. Although Peggy wasn't any closer to understanding her past, she was happy to have met Grandpa and Sarah.

"Thank you for all your help," said Peggy, "I hope we see each other soon."

"You are welcome Peggy," said Grandpa.

"If you ever come to the Cove, be sure to visit."

"We will for sure, won't we Grandpa?" agreed Sarah.

"Yes, my dear. Although we haven't been down your way for many moons, maybe we'll take a trip. I hope you find your past."

"Thanks Grandpa," said Peggy as she and Janet headed down the road to Fraser's homestead.

It was late in the afternoon when they arrived back at Janet's. They came through the side door, which opened directly into the kitchen.

"Well how was your visit?" asked Mrs. Fraser.

"Pretty good," said Peggy who was interrupted by the clock on the mantle. It started to strike four o'clock, but stopped at three dongs.

"Oh my dear, I forgot to wind the clock," said Mrs. Fraser. "Janet, would you and Peggy mind doing it for me? My hands are covered with flour."

"Yes, Ma," replied Janet as she picked up the stool and placed it in front of the couch. For some unknown reason, it was a treat for most children to wind the clock. Janet hoped it would snap Peggy out of her somber mood.

"I'll hold the stool while you lean over the couch and wind the clock, Peggy. Make sure you wind both springs. The one on the left is for the time and the one on the right is for the chime."

Peggy climbed on the stool, opened the clock door and, with the key, wound both sides. Janet could see Peggy was still far away in her thoughts.

The clock didn't work any miracles, nor did anything else that day, or the days that followed. Itching to snap Peggy out of her trance, Janet asked, "Is there anything I can do?"

"No. I'll be fine. Please don't tell anyone about the dreamcatcher until I remember who I am. Visiting Sarah has only made me more curious."

"If that's what you want," agreed Janet.

"It is."

All too soon, it was time to go home, and John arrived with Jake pulling the wagon as usual. As Peggy and John climbed on the wagon, Peggy remembered to be what Mary always told her. "Thanks for having me, Mrs. Fraser. I hope Janet can come visit soon."

"You're welcome, my dear. I'm sure Janet will find an excuse to drop down sooner than you think."

"I hope you're right."

"See you later, Peggy. I hope the dreamcatcher works," said Janet as she smiled.

"Me too," agreed Peggy, who knew Janet meant more than just keeping away nightmares.

Peggy was unusually quiet as she and John started home. John noticed Peggy's attention was focused on the dreamcatcher.

"Tell me, what's so interesting about that dreamcatcher?"

"It's a special gift from Grandpa Knockwood," she replied, and tucked it under her cape. "Anything exciting happen while I was away?" she asked, changing the subject.

"Nothing much. Except Mary trying to scare off a skunk that keeps showing up whenever I'm not around. Every time the neighbours hear a gunshot, they wonder if she had enough nerve to shoot it or not."

"I hope it's far from the house if she does, or we'll have to move out."

"You're right about that," chuckled John.

"Unless the wind blew the stink over to Billy's. That would be good."

"Do you think it would be good for Rosa? She'd have to smell it too."

"Oh yeah. I guess that wouldn't be fair would it. How can she be so nice and Billy so mean?"

"She has more of her mother's temperament."

"Too bad Billy didn't."

"You have to remember, Billy hasn't had an easy life with Tom. I'm sure if his Ma would have been around while he was growing up, he'd be a much happier boy."

"Why did she leave?"

"Tom told her to get out, and never come back. She wanted to take Rosa and Billy, but Tom wouldn't hear of it. He told her Billy was staying."

"Why? Was she a witch?"

"Quite the contrary. It was like she almost worshiped the ground Tom walked on, but when he lost his business, he became a totally different person. He took to the bottle and became bitter and angry. Martha tried every thing she could to stop him from drinking. The harder she tried, the angrier he became. He blamed all his troubles on her nagging and finally kicked her out."

"That's no reason for Billy to act the way he does."

"It was pretty hard on the poor little fellow. He was never the same after she left. Nobody understood why Tom wanted to keep Billy because he ignored him most of the time. When Billy got older, he discovered he got lots of attention by getting into trouble, being a bully and fighting."

"Hmm...I see. It's too bad Mrs. Robertson wouldn't have taken him. Did you ever get in fights when you were young?"

"Now why did you have to ask that question?"

"That means you did, right? Tell me about it."

"You don't need to know about that."

"Yes I do. Now tell me, please!"

"Oh alright. You see, Pa always taught us never to start a fight, but not to run if someone picked on us. 'If you don't stand up for yourself, they'll torture you the rest of your life,' he said."

After a few minutes of silence, Peggy kept prodding.

"You didn't tell me about the fight."

"You were supposed to forget about it."

"I'm not going to forget this one! Come on. Tell me."

"Well there was this big fellow who'd come up behind me, especially on cold days, and ping my ear. It really hurt. At first I told him to lay off, but that didn't stop him. Then one day I had enough. He sneaked up behind me and did it again. Without looking, I swung my arm around, and backhanded him good."

"What happened then?" asked Peggy excitedly.

"The boys said I should have seen the look on his face when my hand connected. He was furious, and told me to put'em up."

"Put up what?"

"My fists, of course."

"Did you?"

"Yes ma'am."

"Then what?"

"He swung, and I ducked. That's when I had my chance."

"For what?" asked Peggy, now immersed in the story.

"Before he knew what happened, I gave him a hard punch straight in the stomach. It knocked the wind right out of him."

"And?" asked Peggy, now bouncing on her seat.

"While he was bent over gasping for air, I spun him around, slipped off his suspenders, and pulled out his shirt. Before he knew it, I had it wrapped it over his head."

"That must have been funny," laughed Peggy.

"He didn't think so," assured John.

"Then what?"

"That's it. I walked away."

"Walked away? Why didn't you give him a good boot in the rear while he was bent over?"

"He got the message."

"What happened after that?"

"Nothing. Never bothered me again. Matter of fact, as time went on we became close friends."

"Who was it?" smiled Peggy.

"Doesn't matter. If it was you, would you want your children to know someone put you in your place?"

"I guess not."

"You could do that to Billy for me, couldn't you?" asked Peggy as she held John's arm and looked deep into his eyes.

"Now you know better than that. Then I'd be the bully. We'll have to find a better way to deal with Billy."

"Well I think it's a good idea," said Peggy, and went back to studying the dreamcatcher.

"I'm sure you do," laughed John as they came over the hill near the big rock called the Whale's Back. They'd soon be home.

To go into the Cove, it was necessary to make a right turn off the main road. Not more than a few hundred feet inside the Cove Road, near the big rock on the left, was a gate that kept the cattle from escaping. Whenever anyone approached, children ran to open and close it, in hopes of a reward for their effort. "Welcome home," smiled Sally and a number of others who were running to greet them and tend to the gate.

"Open and close the gate for me and you can all pile on the wagon for a ride," laughed John. After coming through and closing the gate, they all piled on with delight. Over the brow of the hill, Billy was strutting along while shooting his slingshot at whatever caught his fancy. "Oh, no! Not already," moaned Peggy, "Why did I have to run into him so soon?"

"Hello, Billy, how's she going there?" John asked.

His only answer was a little grunt. As they passed, Peggy looked back over her shoulder. Billy was standing with his slingshot pulled to the limit, aimed straight at her. He let go. Peggy ducked, but nothing happened. The smirk on his face sent the message that she was in for more trouble.

After a hearty welcome home by Mary and the boys, Peter shouted, "You girls want a ride? Pa wants me to take these barrels to the wharf. I'm heading down with Jake."

"We're coming," said Peggy and Sally.

"I just saw Billy going back toward the Cove. I hope you two are getting along," warned Peter.

"Mary told me to stay away from him, if that's what you call getting along."

As they weaved their way to the wharf, Hector circled overhead.

"There's Hector again. I wish I could glide like that. How does he stay motionless in the sky?" asked Peggy.

"By riding the current," laughed Peter.

Suddenly, Hector gave a sharp piercing squeal as he tilted to one side and dropped to the ground where he lay motionless.

Peggy, watching in horror, ran to her precious bird, "Hector, no! No! This can't be!" She picked him up.

Poor Hector. He opened his large yellow beak, but didn,t make a sound. He looked straight at Peggy while his eyes slowly closed. "No, Hector! Don't die!" she begged. "Did anyone see what happened?"

"I didn't see a thing, did you Sally?"

"No, nothing."

"Take him home, and see if Ma can help," suggested Peter.

Hector Gliding

Peggy gently folded Hector's wings, and cradled him in her arms. As she turned, she noticed someone move. It was Billy peeking around the side of his Pa's fish shed. He ducked back out of sight. Peggy's blood boiled.

"It was that Billy and his stupid slingshot. I just know it," she cried. "I'd like to smash it over his head. Maybe that'd knock some sense into him. How can anyone be so cruel and mean?"

"Never mind him now, Peggy. Let's get Hector home," encouraged Sally.

Billy saw Hector's horrific crash and heard Peggy's words. Behind the shed, he thought about tossing his slingshot away, but changed his mind, and shoved it in his back pocket.

As gently as she could, Peggy hurried home, "Mary! Mary! Help me," she yelled, as Sally opened the door. "I think Hector's dying," she sobbed.

"What happened?"

"He was gliding overhead when he just dropped. He had a terrible crash. Look how scratched his poor beak is! I saw Billy with his slingshot. He ducked behind his Pa's fish shed when he saw me looking at him. I just know he did it. Why would he want to kill Hector?" she sobbed.

"Oh dear. Not again," sighed Mary. "And so soon."

"And you told me to be nice to him," cried Peggy.

"We'll discuss Billy later. Let's take care of Hector right now. Here, put him in this box. Hopefully he'll survive. We'll keep an eye on him, but that's all we can do," warned Mary.

"I'm not leaving his side."

"I'll stay with you," said Sally.

"Thanks," replied Peggy, and they sat watching Hector. Sally listened for hours while Peggy whispered about all the things she was going to do to Billy.

As night drew on, Sally said, "I have to go now. I hope Hector is better by tomorrow."

"Thanks Sally. I hope you're right."

Before going to bed, Peter stepped into Peggy's room to check on Hector.

"Is he doing any better?" he asked.

"I don't think so. He's just sitting there with his eyes closed. Once in a while he opens his mouth, but doesn't make a sound."

"I think he'll be better in the morning," Peter assured.

"I'd like you and your friends to teach Billy a lesson. He needs to have some of his own medicine. Why don't you guys show him what it's like to be hurt? Would you do that for me?" asked Peggy.

"Are you kidding? Ma and Pa would find out sooner or later and I'd be severely punished. You'll have to fight this battle yourself."

"Maybe I will!"

It was another night of having a hard time falling asleep, but fatigue eventually did its job. Peggy woke with the sound of a piercing squawk. Forcing open her sleepy eyes, she saw Hector hopping around the floor with his wings outstretched. Peggy woke faster than if a bucket of cold water was doused over her. Her eyes lit up and joy filled her heart. In her excitement, she made a grab for Hector, but he misinterpreted her enthusiasm as an attempt of being captured. That started an awful spell of squawking as he flew toward the window. Wham! Peggy couldn't believe he didn't smash the glass or break his neck.

"Calm down! Calm down!" shouted Peggy, above Hector's scolding shrieks, but he wouldn't listen. He took off in the opposite direction and flew in circles around her room. His wings knocked over her dolls, tipped the lampshade, which smashed on the floor. He ended his flying episode abruptly when he saw another gull invading his territory. He landed on the bureau and attacked violently. Puzzled why the only thing he was hurting was his beak, he finally surrendered, but he kept staring at the unwelcome guest as he look intently in the mirror.

Peggy hurried to open the window so Hector could fly

out, but he misunderstood her intent, and he went into another flying episode. Mary came charging through the door, and poor Hector slammed right into her. It was impossible to know who was more terrorized. He flew to the windowsill where he landed and looked back at the two of them with a mean eye. Then, with his head outstretched, he let out another call as if to say, "Enough of this foolishness, I'm going fishing." and he flew off.

However, his fishing trip ended abruptly when he met Becky, his mate. They circled and chased each other as if they'd been parted for days.

Peggy suddenly felt a twinge of sadness, *I wish I could fly away and be with my family,* she thought.

"I guess Hector is better," Mary exclaimed after the dust had settled.

"Yes, he sure is!"

"Well, thank heavens," Mary sighed. "I think you've had enough trouble for a while. Come along, breakfast is waiting."

After eating and doing her chores, Peggy stepped outside. Hector was perched on the rooftop, but flew off, and circled over Billy's house. He went into another dive. Peggy's heart raced and she tore off towards Billy's fearing the worst. She sighed with relief when Hector shot high into the sky. At that moment, Billy stepped out of the shed with a load of wood. He looked Peggy's way, but pretended he didn't see her.

"Well, there's Mr. Big Shot, himself. It's about time he did something decent. Here's my chance to give him a piece of my mind," mumbled Peggy, and continued marching toward the Robertsons'.

As she rounded the corner of the neglected old shed, shaking with anger, she was ready to pounce on Billy with words that would make him shake in his boots. Her eyes caught sight of a large figure staggering through the door. *Just great! Why did Mr. Robertson have to show up now?* She turned to leave when the loud, gruff voice of Billy's Pa made her stop in her tracks.

"I told you to hurry up, you good for nothin' lout!"

"I'm hurryin' Pa. I'm workin' as fast as I can."

"I'm tryin' to teach you to be tough, boy! I can't believe you let that little shipwreck squirt make such a fool of you!" he scorned, indicating this was the real reason for his anger.

Billy, feeling humiliated and hurt all over again, fired back, "You mean like Ma made a fool of you?"

"Don't you dare sass me like that. I'll teach you to keep that trap of yours shut! Get over here!" screamed Tom, now fuming with rage.

"No, Pa! No! Please! I didn't mean it," Billy pleaded.

"Shut up and don't give me any more lip!"

Oh no, Billy's getting a whipping and all because of me. Peggy fled for home and stopped a minute to catch her breath before charging through the door. The look on her face was one of fear and anxiety.

"What's going on, Peggy? You look like you've seen a ghost," Mary asked with deep concern.

"Mr. Robertson is whipping Billy. He was crying and begging him to stop. It was horrible."

"How do you know? Didn't I warn you to stay away from Billy?"

"Yes, but I didn't listen. I had to make him pay for almost killing Hector. His Pa went into the shed just as I came around the corner. That's when I heard him yelling like a crazy man and giving Billy the whipping. His Pa said I made a fool of Billy. It's all my fault."

"Oh, dear! We were afraid there might be trouble in his home. You must not blame yourself. It really has nothing to do with you. There's a lot more to this than you know."

"Like what?"

"Never mind. We'll see what we can do. In the mean

time, you stay away from Billy and don't say a word about this to anyone. It will only make matters worse."

"I'm sorry. I wish I would have listened to you."

"Well, I'm glad to hear that, young lady," Mary said in a half scolding and a half sympathetic tone. She took Peggy in her arms, wiping her tears away.

"It's no wonder that boy acts the way he does. Inside, he's just plain scared, and being a bully is his way of protecting himself. We never know what others are facing, you know. You just met the Mi'kmaq girl, Sarah, right?"

"What does she have to do with this?"

"The Mi'kmaq have a saying; never judge another person until you walk a mile in their moccasins. There's a lot about Billy and his family that you don't know. Everyone has a story. It doesn't pay to judge anyone too quickly, now does it?"

Peggy, still traumatized, could only utter a subdued, "Yes, ma'am."

That night, when Mary came to say goodnight, Peggy admitted, "I'm thinking about how I should treat Billy."

"Well, there's not a lot you can do, but you could try to be a friend."

"Friend?" protested Peggy. "I feel sorry for him, but that doesn't change what he did."

"Think about whom you have really hurt with your feelings of bitterness."

Peggy struggled with the answer.

"Well, I suppose Billy."

"And who else? Who else benefits from forgiveness? Who's been feeling miserable every time you see him?"

"Me?"

"Yes, of course. If you can understand that, you'll avoid a lot of unnecessary sorrow in your life."

"I don't think I could ever be his friend."

"Remember a few years ago, when Blanche was so mean to you on your very first day at school? She told you to leave, so she and her friends could play hopscotch, and then she made fun of you because you lost your memory."

"Blanche wasn't as mean as Billy."

"That's only because you had her name in the Christmas draw and we learned that she never owned a new doll. Look how nice she was to you the night of the concert, after she opened her gift. She came and thanked you, and then apologized for being so rude."

"Yes, but she kept me from getting soaked one day by walking me home with her umbrella. Billy hasn't apologized or done anything nice for me."

"But you made the first move. I'm asking you to try to do the same with Billy."

"I don't know if I can."

"Do your best. Goodnight, dear."

After much thought, Peggy concluded, *If only Billy would leave the Cove, my problem would be solved, but that's not likely to happen. If I ever do forgive him, he'll have to change*

Chapter 4
Visitors Arrive at the Cove

Early the next morning, there was quite a stir at the Cove. A large ship, the *Flora M*, dropped anchor just off shore. Visitors always brought excitement to the residents of the Cove, especially if the vessels were from distant lands.

The red sky and approaching low black clouds kept the fishermen from heading out to the fishing grounds. They stood around on the wharves surmising why a ship flying a Scottish flag had stopped at the Cove and they expected someone would row ashore any minute. That didn't happen.

A sudden downpour sent every man for shelter in his fish shed, or to his home. Everybody would have to wait to satisfy their curiosity.

Beating rain kept everyone aboard the *Flora M*. It wasn't until sunset the second night that a break under the ridge of clouds indicated the storm had passed.

The following morning, a clear warm day was welcomed by all. John had been out earlier to check his nets and had since returned with his catch. He was cleaning and salting the fish. Peggy helped by spreading salt while John placed the cod in the puncheons.

When they finished, John said, "There you go Peggy. Thanks for your help. Now you're free as a bird."

"Good! I know just what I'm going to do." And up to the loft she went, dug out the old battered telescope, and headed for the entrance to the Cove. After arriving, she sat to investigate the visiting ship when she saw that annoying Billy. *Now what's he up to?* she wondered, the telescope still raised to her eye. *At last, here's my chance to give him a piece of my mind.*

Billy was returning from his fishing trip. Fortunately, he had good luck. A couple of nice cod, half a dozen haddock, and one small halibut topped off his catch. That would put his Pa in a good mood and hopefully stop him from giving Billy any beatings for a while.

Aboard the *Flora M*, Oliver was trying to appease Hannah, who by now was fit to be tied. "I've been cooped up on this wretched ship for far too long Oliver, and I've eaten more eggs and toast than most people devour in a lifetime! Get me something more appetizing now or make yourself useful by holding this stubborn curl in position until it flattens."

"I'm not touching your hair. I'll take my chances on meeting a local fisherman who might have something to satisfy your craving. Surely that'll put you in a better mood," he mumbled as he slithered out.

"For your sake, you better find a delicacy," threatened Hannah.

On deck, Oliver searched the bay in hope of finding someone coming along with Hannah's favourite fish. His attention was attracted to the waves breaking off to the southwest of the point. *What an ominous and dangerous looking thing. Like a rock that could wreck a ship,* he reasoned. That's when he spotted Billy coming around the point, and heading straight for the *Flora M*. Oliver waited with enthusiasm. "Good morning, young man. Were you out fishing bright and early?"

"Yes sir."

"How did you do?"

"Six cod, three haddock, and one halibut."

"Halibut? I'll buy it from you. How much is it worth?"

"It's priceless sir!"

"Nonsense! Everything has a price."

"Pa'd be furious if I sold his favourite fish. I'd hate to think of what he'd do if he found out."

"He doesn't know you caught it, does he? It could be our little secret. Name your price."

"It's not a big one, but I'd say it's worth at least a couple half penny tokens."

"I'll double that."

"Double?" exclaimed Billy while his thoughts raced between the tokens and his Pa putting another beating on him. He studied the Cove; there was no sign of his Pa. He was thinking.

"I see you are hesitating. Don't give it another thought. Come aboard and have eggs and toast with us?"

"Oh I don't think so, sir."

"You would be doing me a great service. My wife hasn't had any social life since we've been on this ship. We are interested in hearing stories of shipwrecks. Surely you know the history of your village?"

"Oh yes, sir. That I do!"

"That looks like a dangerous place over there," said Mr. Knotty, pointing.

"I can tell you all about Halibut Rock," assured Billy.

"Not out here my boy. Come! Let us eat."

"Well..."

"I insist. It would be a pleasure to have you at our table. What's your name, son?"

"Billy, sir. Billy Robertson."

"I'm pleased to meet you, Billy. I'm Barrister Knotty."

Billy was on top of the world. He was bubbling with excitement and couldn't wait to tell everyone how this important man treated him with respect. Breakfast was tempting; he hadn't had more than a crust of bread and molasses along with a few scraps of salted cod since daybreak. He was starved and the thought of eggs and toast made his mouth water.

Billy climbed aboard the *Flora M*, tied his boat, and followed Mr. Knotty to his cabin. Mr. Knotty knocked before entering. "Hannah, we have company. Is it alright if we come in?"

"For heavens sake, Oliver. You know I'm not presentable. Give me a few minutes," she replied in an irritated voice.

"I think I'll leave, sir," said Billy after hearing Hannah.

"No. Please stay. It's alright... Hannah! Let us in."

"What do you mean? Alright," she scolded while opening the door a crack.

"I've met Billy and he has wonderful stories to tell us. I'm sure you will want to hear them," he insisted.

Seeing Billy was only a young lad and nobody important, Hannah opened the door.

"What kind of stories?" she asked.

"Shipwrecks. Like the one we're doing research on," replied Oliver.

"Come in," she relinquished.

Mrs. Knotty looked fine to Billy. He couldn't understand why she complained about not being presentable.

"Billy, this is Mrs. Knotty. Hannah, this is Billy Robertson. Billy knows about every shipwreck along the coast. I've asked him to join us for breakfast."

"It's a pleasure to meet you, Mrs. Knotty."

"I'm sure it is," she replied. "Sit there if you don't mind." She pointed to the opposite end of the table, and filled a plate with eggs and toast. She handed it Oliver to pass along to Billy.

"Thank you ma'am," said Billy as he dove into the food.

"You're welcome," she managed to reply before turning up her nose at the disgusting odor of Billy's fishy clothes and scale-covered hands. She went right to the point, "Have you ever witnessed a shipwreck Billy?"

"Only once. Saw it with my own eyes."

"Really!" gasped Mr. Knotty who leaned closer. "It must have been terrifying."

"Sure was!" Billy replied with his mouth jammed full of eggs and toast.

Billy's crudeness appalled Mrs. Knotty, but Oliver wasn't the least bit concerned. He was priming Billy to find out about the girl, Hope MacEve.

"When did it happen?" questioned Mr. Knotty.

"Only a few years ago."

"That recently? Did anyone survive?" asked Mrs. Knotty, now seeing the advantage of Oliver's discovery.

"Only one."

"What a tragedy. What was his name?" she asked.

"She's a girl!" replied Billy rather disgusted.

"Where was she from, and is she still here?" asked Mrs. Knotty.

"They figure she's from Scotland, but she can't remember a thing, not even her name. Mary named her Peggy."

"Who is Mary?" asked Mrs. Knotty now determined to find Hope.

"Mary and John took her in. Their daughter, Elizabeth, died two years before the wreck. Peggy got all her stuff."

"She must be special to the village. How old is this Peggy?" asked Mrs. Knotty.

"They think she's about eleven or twelve, but I wouldn't call her special."

"Why is that, Billy?" asked Mrs. Knotty, puzzled.

"Because she likes getting me in lots of trouble."

"Maybe if she knew you had a barrister for a friend she'd treat you better," smiled Mr. Knotty. "How will we be able to recognize her?"

"Oh you can't miss her. She's a scrawny thing with dirty blond hair. Everyone talks about her deep blue eyes, but I've seen prettier, and she flaps her tongue so much it's hard to get a word in edgewise."

Mr. Knotty was bubbling.

"You're right Billy, you certainly know a lot. I'd call you a walking history book, wouldn't you, Mrs. Knotty?"

"You took the words right out of my mouth, Oliver."

"Does Peggy live near here?" asked Mr. Knotty.

"She's always too close for me. You can't see her house from here, but I can tell you how to find it, and ours too."

"We'd like that," agreed Mr. Knotty.

Billy gave the Knottys directions for Peggy's home and his. He didn't leave out any details. The Knottys had a clear picture in their minds.

"Is there anything else you'd like to tell us, Billy?" asked Mrs. Knotty. "The more we know, the better our chance to help you."

Billy, enthralled with the attention and sympathy, poured out Peggy's whole story.

"We're sorry you've been so badly treated by this child. If there is anything we can do, just let us know!" assured Mrs. Knotty who managed to give Billy a pat on the shoulder as she took his empty plate and turned away her nose.

"Thanks a lot. I'll remember that. Well, I better be headin' in now. Thanks for the breakfast."

"You're more than welcome, Billy. Do visit us again. We may be here for several days," encouraged Mr. Knotty.

"I certainly will," said Billy as Mr. Knotty led him through the door and onto the deck. Billy began to untie his boat, when he had a second thought.

"Ah...maybe I'll sell that halibut after all. Just don't breathe a word about it to anyone."

"Agreed," smiled Mr. Knotty, and handed Billy a couple of one-penny tokens.

"Wow! Thanks Mr. Knotty," said Billy as he shoved off.

"You're welcome, Billy," said Mr. Knotty as they parted.

Oliver was cheered by the information Billy had given them and he returned to the cabin.

"Hannah, I think we should go ashore to become acquainted with certain folks. I would like to find this

Peggy of the Cove and assess the situation. I think we've struck the motherlode."

"I agree, but what concerns me is how you're going to convince her new family to give her up to us without a fuss."

"I'm working on that."

"I bet you are."

When Billy left the *Flora M* and came through the entrance of the Cove, Peggy was still waiting, "So there's Mr. Big Shot himself! I suppose you're really proud that you hit Hector with your slingshot! Do you think that's going to make you a man?"

"You can't prove a thing. How is the old bird anyway? I haven't seen him lately."

"He's not an old bird and he's fine, no thanks to you!"

"You need to get your facts straight. You can't prove it was me. Maybe the next time he's around, I'll take a shot and it won't be to wing him."

"You stay away from Hector. I remember seeing the guilt written all over your face. You told on yourself!"

"You? Remember? That's a laugh. You don't even know who you are. You're just imagining things again. Besides, Hector should have his wings clipped after dive-bombing me."

Peggy exploded.

"You inconsiderate brute. I might have accepted your apology if you had come clean, but not now. I can't believe I thought there might be one decent bone in that miserable body of yours. I was wrong about that too," shouted Peggy with arms swinging.

"Why are your arms flying around? You wanna hit me or something?"

"I'd do more than hit if I could get my hands on you."

"I'll let you hit me all you want if you swim out to the boat."

"Go home where you belong!"

"What's the matter? You chicken? Cluck! Cluck! Cluck! I

knew it. Peggy's scared of the water, nah, nah, nah-ah!"

"Why don't you just leave the Cove? Go away! Nobody wants you around here anyway."

Billy shuddered at Peggy's words, but covered his feelings by retaliating.

"Well I'll have you know some people appreciate me, like those nice rich people on the *Flora M.* They even invited me back."

"That's because they don't know the truth...aaaah!" answered Peggy in disgust, too frustrated to say another word.

"They know the truth about you."

"You don't know what the word 'truth' means and what business did you have talking about me?"

"I'll have you know they invited me aboard to have breakfast with them. They treated me like a king. That's more than I can say for you. Why don't you go visit them, maybe they'll be able to teach you how to appreciate people like me!"

"You're the one who needs to be taught; you're a nobody the way you behave."

"Not according to them. I told them all about you and your temper. They know you're a spoiled brat!"

"You didn't!"

"I sure did and they feel some bad for me. Matter of fact, they asked a lot about you and I told them *everything!* So, now what do you have to say for yourself?"

"If I told them everything about you, they'd treat you like a criminal. What did they want to know about me anyway?"

"If you were the famous 'Peggy of the Cove,'" he said in a sophisticated high voice with his nose in the air, wagging his head.

"Why would they care? Who are they?" Peggy asked, now becoming curious about their interest in her.

"He's a barrister and his wife is one fine lady. And they invited me back any time I want. How do you like that?"

Peggy was trying to add up the facts while arguing

with Billy. Could it be that these strangers were searching for *her?* Her heart pounded at the thought of making contact with her lost family. Questions flashed through her mind. When would these strangers come ashore? Maybe they were her Mama and Papa. They couldn't be. They wouldn't have waited for the rain to stop. She was overwhelmed. What will Mary do? Excitement and fear gripped her trembling body. There was only one way to find out.

"I've had enough of this, I'm leaving," said Peggy as she picked up the old telescope and started off.

"Whatcha doin' with that telescope? Spying on me or something?"

"That'd be a waste of time. Anyway, it's none of your business!"

"If you don't keep out of my life, it's my business," warned Billy.

"That's the most intelligent thing I ever heard you say and that's exactly what I want to do, stay out of your life. And I want you to stay out of mine," demanded Peggy.

"Yeah well, make sure you do," shouted Billy, wanting to have the last word.

Peggy never answered, but hurried back to the loft, pondering why those strangers were asking about her. She was still fuming, and wished Billy would hurry up and finish cleaning his fish, and get out of her sight. Every time she looked out the window, there he was, smiling and whistling like he owned the world. She wanted to go down and smack him again with another cod. She even imagined Hector watching. He'd smile his best seagull smile, or at least joyfully squeal, seeing her sweet revenge. At last, Billy left and it wasn't until she heard one of the boys yell, "Look who's coming!" that she was able to focus on something other than Billy.

Everyone gathered to meet the mysterious visitors. Rosa was among the young people who squeezed to the front for a better look. As Mr. and Mrs. Knotty climbed onto the wharf, they both spotted Rosa. Between the portrait and Billy's description, Mr. Knotty was convinced. "You must be the famous Peggy of the Cove," he proudly admitted with great confidence, as he looked straight at Rosa. All the kids laughed, knowing full well this stranger didn't have a clue what he was talking about.

Rosa covered up a giggle while shrinking back from Mr. Knotty's gaze, and the children's resounding snickers. She wrung her fingers into her skirt, letting go only to push strands of her straight blond hair from her eyes.

Mr. Knotty, with growing bewilderment, looked across the laughing children's faces and listened to their gleeful twittering mingled with whispers from behind cupped hands.

Hannah leaned to Oliver's ear and whispered, "I don't think this is the girl."

Oliver looked again at Rosa, and was about to speak when he was cut off by an angry male voice.

"Rosa!"

Immediately the laughter stopped.

Rosa's expression grew stony. She tensed her jaw and turned to see her Pa standing behind her, his expression humorless.

Drawn by the shout, Oliver too had looked to see the man. At his side, browbeaten, and with his hands shoved in his pockets, stood Billy. As Oliver stared toward Billy, the boy averted his look to the ground.

"Get over here!" roared Tom to Rosa. He made a gesture for her to come to him.

With barely a glance to the other children, Rosa hurried toward her Pa.

Oliver watched the way Rosa kept straight ahead when she passed her Pa and Billy, not once did she meet her Pa's glare as it bore down upon her.

When Rosa had passed, her Pa turned to look straight at Oliver.

Oliver, with a sudden flush of self-consciousness, broke his gaze and looked away to the village as though to gain his bearings. He stuck out his beard in an air of dignity, straightened his lapels, and took a breath.

"Shall we walk dear?" he said to Hannah.

The Knottys casually walked through the village, past the church, and on to the gate. Oliver made sure he kept his eye on the house that Billy described as Peggy's and the Robertson home. Satisfied beyond doubt, he wanted to put his plan into action immediately. He couldn't resist the temptation any longer. He wanted to pry about Peggy.

"Come, Hannah, let's see what we can discover," he insisted with eagerness.

"Aren't you being a little hasty? Are you sure you're ready?" asked Hannah.

"Positive my dear. Besides, I have more than one idea. It's becoming more appealing to me by the minute, you watch and see."

The Knottys approached the door of Mary's home. As Oliver confidently knocked, his nostrils inhaled the mouth-watering aroma, "My! It sure smells good in here. You must be the best cook in town," he greeted Mary.

"Thank you, sir," she replied, smiling as her face became a little warm. "May I help you?"

"I'm Barrister Oliver Knotty and this is my wife, Mrs. Knotty. May we have a word with you?"

"Why, of course, do come in. Have a seat."

"Thank you, Mrs. ..."

"Mary. Just call me Mary."

"Well, Mary, I have been appointed to investigate the disappearance of a ship. Over three years ago, the *Little Miss Fortune* sailed from Scotland, and hasn't been heard from since.

The ship had a stopover at Plymouth, so some claim she sailed from England. Word has come back that a shipwreck occurred here and only a little girl survived. We believe she is Hope MacEve. I've been assigned to take her back to Scotland. Rumor has it you are caring for such a child."

Mary's cheerful countenance and high spirits sank like

an anchor to the depths of the sea. Her mind raced for solutions, while trying to remain calm.

"I'd like to see proof that you have been sent here to find this lost child."

"If you insist," said Mr. Knotty with confidence, and rather smartly pulled an envelope from his suit pocket, opened it, and slapped the papers on the table. "There! See? It's all legal."

Mary picked up the document. She studied it for a few minutes, and with dread in her eyes, placed it on the table. "What do you know about this girl?" she asked in a defensive tone.

"She was eight years old at the time, blue eyes, fair complexion, and long blond hair; at least it was then. You may detect a slight Scottish accent, but since she also lived in Europe and traveled extensively with her folks, it's not that noticeable."

"Why would you want to take her back to Scotland?"

"I need proof that the girl in question is indeed Hope before I disclose that information. You understand, of course."

"No, I do not," Mary answered abruptly, while leaving the table to place a log on the fire.

"We wouldn't want imposters claiming to be Hope's relatives."

"Imposters? Please explain."

"Somebody might want to keep her as their own."

"Yes, of course. What about her parents?"

"They were on the ship, so we assume they were lost."

"If she doesn't have family, why take her back to Scotland?"

"There are relatives."

"What sort of folks are they? Poor, rich, or what?"

By now, Mr. Knotty felt Mary was getting too close to the truth, and wanted to avoid any further questions. He was looking for a way out. "I wouldn't exactly call them poor."

"If her relatives are rich, maybe they just want her for

an inheritance or worse, marry the innocent child to some old baron," suggested Mary.

"That is preposterous!" assured Mr. Knotty, trying to get away from the truth.

Mary sensed something was amiss when the barrister became irritated and avoided looking her in the eye. It was a dead give-a-way.

"I'm sorry, but I don't believe I can be of any help. Why don't you return to Scotland, and tell the authorities you were unable to find this Hope MacEve?" she insisted as she pointed to the door.

"Not until I investigate thoroughly. Don't be surprised if we visit again," assured Mr. Knotty. "Thank you for your time. Good day," he said as he reached to take his papers that Judge Sampson had given him.

Mary snatched the document in the nick of time and without warning, quickly stepped to the stove, and threw the papers into the fire. "That's what I think of your legality. Now please leave my house!" she instructed in a harsh voice.

"You can be charged for destroying that document," warned Mr. Knotty. " We're not leaving until we find Hope." His face was red with anger and he was pointing his finger right in front of Mary's nose while threatening her.

"Hannah, let's search the house. I believe she's hiding Hope MacEve."

"Leave my house at once!" shouted Mary, but the Knottys paid no attention and headed for the living room to begin their search.

In a frenzy, Mary entered the pantry, grabbed the old musket, loaded it, and marched in behind the Knottys. "Get out now or I'll pull the trigger," she threatened while aiming between Mr. Knotty's eyes.

"Don't be so foolish. Put that musket down," ordered Mr. Knotty, now trembling.

"Not until you're out of my house. Now move!"

"I'll have you arrested for attempted murder."

"Out!" shouted Mary as she entered the parlor, leaving the doorway free for them to escape. When Mr. Knotty hesitated, she stuck the musket against his back and pushed. "I won't push the second time. If you don't leave now, they'll be dragging you out," warned Mary in a shaky voice.

"Come Hannah, the woman's gone mad," exclaimed Mr. Knotty. "We'll have the law take care of her."

With that, Oliver took Hannah by the hand and hurried outside. Mary followed close behind with the musket breathing down Mr. Knotty's neck.

A short distance from the house, Hannah scolded Oliver. "You should have grabbed that musket and smashed it."

"Yes and had my brains blown out."

"Sometimes you're such a coward," and with that, Mrs. Knotty turned to face Mary, advancing toward her as if to attack.

"Get back," warned Mary, as once again she raised the musket.

"Don't you tell me what to do!" scorned Mrs. Knotty.

With that, Mary took aim and fired. The loud report echoed down through the Cove, the shot brushing past Mrs. Knotty's feet. She made a wild dash back to Oliver.

"You're right, the woman's mad. Let's get out of here!"

"And don't darken my doorstep again," threatened Mary. "There'll be no warning the next time."

Hearing gunshots in and around the Cove was normal. If wildlife strayed near any home, it made for an easy meal. So most people paid no attention when they heard Mary's shot, but one neighbour couldn't resist. He knew about the skunk that was plaguing Mary's life. He stuck his head around the corner of his house and asked, "Did you have the nerve to shoot that skunk this time Mary, or just scare him off again?"

"Scared them off."

"Them! You mean there's more than one now?" he asked. "Is that who you were yelling at?"

"Yes! There were two of them, but I don't think they'll be back."

"How's that?" asked the neighbour.

"I think they'll pass the word along. Scared them half to death. You should have seen them run," replied Mary. "That's the last warning."

"If those skunks understand words, they'll stay away," laughed her neighbour.

"Oh they understand alright," assured Mary.

After a good distance from Mary's, Hannah started needling Oliver again.

"Sometimes you don't make a very good liar, Oliver. I wanted to tell you to smarten up when Mary started questioning you about the MacEves being rich."

"I don't need any criticism. You could have helped by changing the subject you know."

"You're the one who is supposed to be calm under pressure."

"I am in court. This was new territory. I'll be prepared the next time," guaranteed Oliver.

"We can't let Mary know about that inheritance or we'll never get that money. How are you going to persuade them to let Peggy accompany us to Scotland after Mary's outburst that practically killed me?"

"I'm working on that one," Oliver replied, while staring off in deep thought.

"I bet Frank could do it. If you're as clever as he is, you'll find a way."

"As clever! I'm smarter. The only reason he became a judge was because of his connections. I'm far more intelligent! Some day you'll see."

"Well, I'm waiting," taunted Hannah.

"Not for long, my dear. I can outsmart him any day."

"Is that so? He's made a fool of you more than once, and you haven't pulled the wool over his eyes yet."

"You can't count those silly little incidents. I'm thinking that plan B is our only alternative."

"Rosa."

"Well she looks just like Peggy, doesn't she? Billy's never mentioned his Ma. Maybe she's not here or dead. We must convince Mr. Robertson how well-off Rosa will be with us. If he hesitates, surely money will persuade him."

"Sometimes I wonder about you, Oliver! But you just might be right for once."

"I think Rosa would make a wonderful Hope MacEve. I'm sure even your smart chum, Judge Sampson won't know the difference. You'll finally admit I outsmarted him."

"I could bat my eyelashes at him when he looks at Rosa. That would satisfy him in a hurry," she teased.

"Don't you dare! I'll take care of Sampson," insisted Oliver.

"Finding Rosa was purely a stroke of luck. What would you have done if she wasn't here?"

"Huh! A stroke of luck! I had the idea of finding a substitute in the back of my mind long before we came to the Cove. I work on a case as it unravels and since this has fallen into my lap, I don't need another plan."

"You still haven't convinced me it wasn't luck, but we should visit Mr. Robertson."

"It's about time you finally agreed with me. Now let's return to the *Flora M.*"

After dinner, when Peggy was helping to clean up, Mary gave the warning, "Peggy, there's something mysterious about those visitors on the *Flora M.* I want you to stay away from them."

"Why? What have they done?"

"It's a private matter. From what I know, I don't feel good about the whole situation, so I'm asking you to avoid them, even if they approach you. Please don't speak to them."

Peggy didn't answer, she just became more curious. Throughout the remainder of the day, she kept her eye on the Cove, and the *Flora M.* After supper, Sally came to play until dusk. When it was time to leave, Peggy told Mary, "I'm going to walk with Sally to her place, I'll be back later."

"Alright, dear." Mary replied. "Don't be too late."

As the night drew on, Peggy noticed the Knottys coming ashore. It was getting dark, but they had a lantern at the bow of their boat. Now was her chance. "I have to go now, Sally. See you tomorrow."

"Bye, and let's think of some exciting things we can do tomorrow."

"That's a good idea, alright," agreed Peggy as she strolled down the path. She waited until the Knottys passed and were well ahead of her. She was curious why they were coming ashore at night. Were they looking for her, to reunite her with her family? She wanted to catch up to them and ask if she was the one they were looking for, but Mary's warning stuck in her head. She followed closer, hoping to hear their conversation. Even if they turned around, they still wouldn't be able to recognize her in the dark.

Then the heart-sickening blow struck.

"Isn't that the Robertson home?" Peggy heard Mrs. Knotty ask her husband.

"Yes, my dear. We're here," he answered in a joyful, but devious voice.

Holding back the tears of disappointment, Peggy's dream was crushed. She realized something was amiss; the Knotty's weren't the least bit interested in uniting her with her family. They turned onto the path leading to Billy's. Peggy slowed her pace, isolating herself from them, but not for long.

She sneaked behind Tom's shed to wait, and find out what would happen.

A lantern, hanging by the window in the shed, indicated Tom was in his favourite drinking spot. Tucked away in a corner, the old couch provided comfort, as well as privacy, from anyone passing his door. It was a known fact: this was Tom's hideaway. During the winter the old stove kept him warm. He claimed to be working on projects, but everyone knew it was his drinking, more than woodworking, that occupied his time. Most often his tools lay idle while he indulged in his vice.

Mr. Knotty knocked on the door of the Robertsons'. Rosa answered.

"Would your Papa be here?" he asked politely.

"Sort of..." hesitated Rosa while glancing toward the shed.

Before Barrister Knotty had a chance to answer, a gruff voice bellowed from the open door of the nearby shed.

"What d' ya want, mister?"

"Oh! Mr. Robertson, I'm Barrister Knotty and this is my wife, Mrs. Knotty," he said as they walked toward Tom.

"What's on your mind this time of night?" he growled.

"May we have a word with you?"

"You tryin' to get somethin' from me?"

"Oh no, sir. We have good news. May we discuss our proposal?"

"I s'pose so."

Peggy crouched to the little cat door, which offered the ideal spot for eavesdropping. The hole was covered with a piece of canvass to keep out the cold and wind. From there, she could hear any conversation clearly, without being seen.

"Have a seat here on my couch," offered Tom. "What's on your mind?"

"Thank you, Mr. Robertson," said Oliver as he brushed a spot for Hannah. An old, stained couch wasn't their usual seating.

"The friendliness of you folk along the coast has caught our attention. We have an opportunity of a lifetime for your daughter. Our aging housekeeper is retiring and we think your Rosa would fit into her role nicely. Would you agree to her joining us?"

"Rosa! What do you know about her?"

"She was on the wharf this morning when we arrived. We enquired about her and the folks gave nothing but praise."

"Is that so? Well Rosa cleans the house an' does the cookin'. Na, I don't think so!"

"She would receive payment and a proper education. Isn't that what you want for her? We could try it for a year. If she didn't like Scotland, she could return."

"Rosa doesn't need any schoolin' to clean an' cook," Tom argued. "An' who d'ya think you are, tellin' me what's best for Rosa?"

"Of course, Mr. Robertson. You are right. How rude of me," replied Mr. Knotty.

So far, Tom wasn't biting. Mrs. Knotty couldn't take it any longer. It was time to bring on the charm.

"Of course we didn't expect you to let Rosa go for nothing. We plan to pay a hefty sum...say two gold guineas?" she suggested with a pleasant smile designed to melt Tom's heart.

Tom's eyes lit up. They knew by his reaction that they had struck the right cord.

"Nope, I wouldn't even consider less than four. Rosa's a fine worker. I'd have to think twice about lettin' 'er go."

"I see you drive a hard bargain, Mr. Robertson. If Rosa is as good as you say, we'll consider that sum. Excuse us while we go outside to discuss the matter."

Peggy had to act fast. Realizing they would see her, she quickly tiptoed behind the bark pot, and ducked out of sight. To her horror, the Knottys stood on the other side of the pot, only a few feet away. Fortunately, they set the lantern on the ground. Dark long shadows hid her from them. Her body stiffened and she remained breathless while she listened.

"What do you think, my dear? Should we give in or try for a lower price?" asked Oliver.

"Pretend it's too much. We can't look anxious. You saw how he sparkled when money was mentioned. I think he's playing games. Try for three guineas. It's a small token in comparison to what we'll gain," whispered Mrs. Knotty.

"You're right. We must get Rosa. I know that Judge Sampson will never know the difference. Think about it. If you held that portrait of Hope and placed it beside Rosa, wouldn't you be convinced she was Hope?"

"We can't do that, but I see your point. I must have a better look at the portrait when we get back on board," agreed Hannah. "Let's not keep Mr. Robertson waiting."

Peggy sat stunned, a thousand questions racing through her head. She crept back to her listening spot.

"Mr. Robertson, three guineas is a great deal of money. We feel that's the best we can do," said Mr. Knotty, shifting as if about to leave.

"Fine by me," replied Tom without blinking an eye.

"Oliver, I think Mr. Robertson is a very reasonable man. Four guineas it is, Mr. Robertson. May we shake on that?" asked Mrs. Knotty as she reached for Tom's hand to seal the deal.

"You're a clever lady. You should pay close attention to 'er, Barrister."

"I will," agreed Mr. Knotty, not wanting to stir the pot at this opportune moment.

"Thank you for your time, Mr. Robertson. We'll come by tomorrow to make the arrangements," assured Mrs. Knotty.

Both parties rubbed their hands together when out of the others' sight. Each thought they had outdone the other and that only the four of them knew of the deal. The Knottys had no idea Peggy was lurking in the shadows. Peggy remained hidden and out of sight until the Knottys had left.

When she knew it was safe, Peggy crept away, but footsteps were gaining on her. "Who's there?"

No reply.

She quickened her pace. So did the footsteps. She knew it was time to catch her stalker.

At the corner of her path and the road was a large rock. John kept a pole there to chase cattle if they ever broke through the fence. Peggy ducked behind the rock, grabbed the pole, and held it about six inches above the ground. As the intruder approached, she held the pole steady. "Yow!" yelled a familiar voice as he tumbled headfirst.

"What d'ya think you're doin', tryin' to kill me?" scolded Billy, brushing off the dirt and rubbing his skinned hands and knees.

"Don't blame me. You're the one who didn't answer. Tried to scare me, didn't you? When are you going to learn not to mess with me?"

"I thought you might scream. I didn't want Pa to know I was out there. That's why I didn't answer!"

"What do you want, anyway?" demanded Peggy.

Billy stuttered, trying to find his words. "Umm...it's umm... a..."

Peggy wanted to tell him she didn't have all night, but seeing him lost for words was a new experience. By chance, he just might have a speck of remorse in that brain of his.

"I don't know how to help Rosa. I was wondering if you had any ideas?"

"Why should I help you after the stunts you pulled on me and poor Hector? Why did you want to kill him anyway?"

"I'm asking you to help Rosa," he said sadly. "And I didn't try to kill Hector."

"You actually care about someone besides yourself. I find that hard to believe."

"I have feelings too. More than you know."

"Yeah! Hate feelings."

"That's where you're wrong."

"Prove it."

Billy hesitated. "Well...ahh...Oh what's the use? You wouldn't believe me anyway. Forget it," he mumbled and started walking away.

"Try me," dared Peggy, becoming more curious.

"Promise you won't say a word to anyone."

"Oh alright! What is it?"

Billy paused. The silence was deadly.

"I don't have all night."

"Well...I didn't mean to hit Hector. I only meant to scare him. I'm glad he didn't die."

Although a lame apology, at least Billy made an effort, but Peggy wasn't finished testing him yet.

"Why do you want me to help Rosa?"

"Look how good you have it with John and Mary. Rosa deserves the same. I think the Knottys will make Rosa their little slave," he sighed, and turned to wipe his eyes. He didn't know Peggy could see his silhouette against the light from Tom's window.

Maybe Billy has a tiny heart after all, she thought before answering.

"It's me the Knottys want, not Rosa."

"How'd you come up with that dumb idea? Your name wasn't even mentioned. It's Rosa they want. You heard every word they said!"

"Yes, but you couldn't hear them whispering over by the bark pot. They're searching for a young girl who was shipwrecked. They think it's me. Those people are cheaters and liars. Why don't you do something to stop them and help Rosa?"

"It's not that simple," Billy replied, sadly. "I hate to see her leave and I don't trust the Knottys, but she might be better off. It can't get much worse with Pa. She's only been home a while, and I know she hates the way he treats her."

"I'm sorry. I had no idea he was mean to her too. I should have guessed though, knowing the way he treats you."

"I just thought everyone knew," he said sorrowfully. "Rosa would be better off if those Knottys treat her right. Just as soon as they left, Pa told her to pack because she was going away early in the morning."

"Early in the morning! That's so soon!"

"Yeah, but what can I do?"

"I don't know, but try to think of something between now and tomorrow morning. I will too."

"I'll try," said Billy sadly, and with his head down, he left. Peggy could hear his scuffed steps as he slowly trod toward home.

At her place, Peggy sat on the step, gazing at the stars,

wishing Janet were visiting. She'd have good advice. Making tough decisions alone was taking its toll. She remained there weighing the pros and cons until she pretty well made up her mind. One thing she knew for sure, the Knottys must be stopped from leaving early in the morning.

She went inside to the parlor where Mary was knitting, John was reading, and Peter and Joe were playing Chinese checkers. She sat on the sofa between Mary and John. Mary noticed a strange look on her face.

"Is something wrong, my dear? You look worried. Are you having more problems?"

"Sort of. I was talking to Billy on my way home."

"Talking or arguing?"

"Talking."

"Well, I'm glad to know you and Billy are staying on good terms. Or are you?"

"Somewhat, I suppose."

"Good, let's keep it that way."

"He and Rosa don't have it easy, do they?"

"Not really. I hope things get better for them."

"You know, I could have ended up in a family like that. I'm really glad to be here. I love you all," she said, and leaned on Mary's shoulder.

"We all love you too, Peggy. You're one of us, and you have brought joy back into our home after we lost Elizabeth. You know how James adores you. I know those two wouldn't admit it," she said, pointing to Peter and Joe, "but they love you dearly."

"Aw, Ma, cut it out," said Peter. "Sometimes you get all mushy."

Peggy remained cuddled to Mary for some time.

"I'm going to bed," she said, and gave Mary and John a kiss.

"I'll be up in a few minutes, dear," assured Mary.

The best Peggy could do for Peter and Joe was tickle them and pull their nose and ears.

"Oh why not," she said, and gave each of them a peck

on the cheek. "There! Just in case you haven't been kissed, remember, I gave you your first one. Good night everyone."

"Yuck!" replied Peter, who quickly wiped his cheek. Then without warning, he jumped up, forced Peggy's arms over her head and yelled, "Get her Joe!"

After a good tickling they let her go.

"Now that's only a taste of what you'll get if you ever do that again," warned Peter with a big silly grin. "You remember that, now good night!"

Peggy climbed the stairs, but not with the happy bounce she normally had.

"Something's on her mind, John, she's acting strange again."

"She was fine this morning. Maybe she's worn out and needs a good sleep. Wait'n see how she's doing in the morning. Don't lose any sleep over it."

Peggy was in bed when Mary came and tucked her in, but the last thing on her mind was sleep.

Chapter 5
Peggy's Drastic Measure

Peggy lay awake in bed, wrestling with Rosa's predicament and Billy's remorse. She analyzed the conversation the Knottys had about the portrait. If Mr. Knotty believed Judge Sampson would be certain that Rosa was Hope MacEve, why did Mrs. Knotty want to have a second look? What was their purpose in deceiving the Judge? Why did they ask Billy so many questions and then totally ignore her? *I wish I could see that portrait,* Peggy thought, *but how?* She knew the Knottys would be picking up Rosa early in the morning. That would be her only chance to sneak aboard the *Flora M* to see that portrait. She needed more time. Somehow the Knottys must be stopped. She must see that portrait.

Impatiently, Peggy waited until she was convinced everyone was sound asleep. She quietly tied her bed sheets together, attached one end to the leg of her bed, and lowered the other out through the window. Carefully crawling out, she slid down the sheets to reach the trellis, and made her way safely to the ground.

The first quarter of the new moon gave just enough light to find her way in the dark. She made sure each step was on solid footing to avoid any stumbles. At the wharf she took John's splitting knife, which was always stuck in the splitting table, made her way down the ladder, and climbed into the small punt.

Rowing in the dark was a new experience. Placing the oars at the right angle to avoid any splashing noise was a struggle. Gently she rotated each oar until both were in the proper position. She began to row.

It was cooler than she had expected. Before leaving, the thought of going downstairs to get her coat entered her mind, but it was too chancy. Now she wished she had. Thick damp fog that was drifting around the point moistened her clothes, sending shivers through her body.

Once outside the safety of the Cove, the mission didn't seem like such a good idea. Fear of drowning almost forced Peggy to abandon her plan. Before changing her mind, she looked over her shoulder, and there looming in the mist like a huge monster, swayed the *Flora M*. Drawing near the ship's bow, she was met with a threatening glare from the figurine. It was like a warning to abandon her dangerous undertaking. Peggy struggled with her decision, but with no other options, forged ahead.

Quietly, she grabbed the anchor rope, leaned over and began cutting. The job should have taken only seconds, but the knife was so dull it barely cut. It was a mystery. John always kept his knives sharp. Her arm began to wear out.

Between the swells and tide, Peggy struggled to keep her balance. A creaking noise descended from above. Breathless, she looked up. Nobody appeared. It was the squeaking of the rigging, caused by a huge swell. Back to the task, she wondered if the knife would ever cut through the thick rope. Then, without warning, everything let loose.

The sudden drop of the heavy rope yanked Peggy out of the boat, and headfirst into the water, which gushed through her nose and down her windpipe. The mishap brought on a spree of coughing and gulping. Screaming for help was her first impulse, but that would be a dead giveaway. She thrashed about trying to reach the punt before drowning. *Where is it?*, she pleaded, in a desperate attempt to locate the small boat. Swirling in circles, she caught sight of it drifting away, almost out of sight.

Her shoes and clothing were dragging her down, making it almost impossible to swim. At the point of exhaustion, she reached the punt, flung her arms to seize the gunnels, and rested. Numerous attempts to crawl aboard failed. One last desperate effort proved useless. Her weakened body slowly began to sink. She cried, believing her life was over for doing this wicked deed. Kelp brushed against her feet, as if trying to tangle and prevent her escape.

With a prayer, Peggy inhaled what she considered her last breath, when terror turned to hope. She felt the punt bump onto a rock, and then her feet touched it. The slippery kelp and seaweed made it almost impossible to get a solid footing, but eventually she succeeded. In slow motion, she leaned over the gunnels before rolling to the bottom of the boat.

"Thank you, God. I'm going to live," she whispered joyfully while lying there exhausted.

However, her joy didn't last. Questioning her radical mission occupied her thoughts. *Am I going crazy? What if the* Flora M *sinks and everyone drowns? I could be locked up for murder or worse, be hung.* She pictured herself in front of the Judge and jury, pleading, "I didn't mean to kill anybody. I was trying to save Rosa's life. It was an accident. I'm no murderer."

After convincing herself the calm sea would gently cradle the *Flora M* safely on shore, she crawled to the seat, and began rowing back home. It was a chilling experience for two reasons; her cold wet clothes, and the extreme action she had taken. By the time she made it to the wharf, her body was trembling. Quickly, she tied the punt and crept up the hill to the house. Her quiet steps sounded like loud voices tattle tailing stories of her misdeed.

Standing below her window, she wondered if she had enough strength to climb back into her room. Once stationed on the trellis, an idea struck. She tied a couple of knots in the sheet to keep her hands and feet from slipping. The climb to her window was painfully slow, and a struggle, but finally she made it.

In bed, still shivering and shaking, Peggy's thoughts traveled back to her rescue. John had raced her to the nearest home where ladies changed her from wet clothing into a warm, soft nightgown. Mary had wrapped blankets around her before sitting close to the stove with a roaring fire. What she wouldn't give for that right now.

It was getting close to morning before she finally fell asleep, but it was far from a refreshing one.

All too soon, excited voices from the men outside and Peter and Joe downstairs woke her. She had her ear to the crack of the door listening.

"Ma, the *Flora M* is still aground, but the tide's coming in. You should see her. Lucky it was a calm night or there would have been another wreck!" shouted Peter.

"Not so loud, Peter. You'll wake Peggy. Was anyone hurt or the ship damaged?" enquired Mary.

"Doesn't look like it," replied Joe. "Pa and all the other men hope to pull her off when the tide is high."

"Phew! Thank heavens nobody was hurt," Peggy sighed with relief and prepared to get on with her plans. She slipped her wet clothes under the bed, dressed, and headed downstairs.

As she entered the kitchen, Mary exclaimed, "My dear! Peggy, what a mess your hair is, and your eyes are all bloodshot. Do you have a fever?" she asked in alarm as she felt Peggy's forehead. "You don't feel warm. Do you have the chills? Are you coming down with something?"

"I didn't sleep a whole lot last night, but I'm not sick, I can guarantee that."

"Are you sure?"

"Yes."

"Well, if you feel ill later, let me know immediately."

"I will, but I'm not sick."

Peter and Joe, still excited, were coming up with all sorts of speculations about the *Flora M*. Peggy remained silent, except for one question, "Does anyone know how it happened?"

"Nope! But the anchor line was cut," exclaimed Peter. "Everyone in the Cove is wondering why someone did it."

I know why, thought Peggy, and almost said it out loud. She bit her tongue in the nick of time and remained quiet while eating breakfast and doing her chores. When she finished, she told Mary, "I'm going down to the wharf to see what's going on."

"Fine, but remember; if you start feeling chilled or hot, come straight home. Do you understand?"

"Yes, now please relax Mary, for the third time, I'm not sick."

As Peggy headed down to the Cove, she was overjoyed at what she saw. The *Senora* had arrived and was dropping anchor just outside the Cove, away from the *Flora M*. James was home safe and sound.

James was the oldest of Mary and John's three boys and worked as a crewman aboard the *Senora* with Captain Simms. He started the summer following Peggy's shipwreck. He and Peggy bonded the very first day they had met. She helped fill the void he felt when his only sister, Elizabeth, died. Peggy knew she could trust his advice and confided in him whenever she was troubled. She ran to the wharf and waited until he came ashore.

"James! Am I glad to see you! I was beginning to worry after you didn't show up."

"We weren't more than a week late. You know that's not unusual."

"You know me though. I thought the worst. Why is Captain Simms staying here?"

"He's not. He's over at Big Tancook Island and he left me in charge of the *Senora*. We had to load on supplies at the head of the Bay yesterday. We'll pick him up in four or five days. Captain Simms wanted to see how well I could handle the *Senora* without him. Winkle is the only one staying on board."

Winkle was from Upper Hammonds Plains, where his family came to settle after being freed from slavery in Virginia. Lumbering and barrel-making didn't satisfy his yearning like the sea did, so he left the family business, and was happy to land a job with Captain Simms. Being a young, strong man with a good sense of humor made him a pleasant co-worker. He was ambitious and he pleased the Captain with his business capabilities. He was always on the lookout for new opportunities.

"What about the rest of the crew?" asked Peggy.

"We dropped them off after loading the supplies. They'll meet us here before we set sail. It was so calm last night; we practically drifted from Shut-In-Island to here. I was beginning to wonder if we'd ever make it home."

"Wow! That means you're sort of the Captain. You must be proud!"

"It's pretty exciting."

"I wish I had something to be excited about. James, I'm in deep trouble, and I need your help."

"You? In deep trouble? That's a joke!"

"It's no joke this time. I'm serious."

"What did you do? Set that ship adrift?" he replied like it was the last thing on earth Peggy would do.

Gulp! thought Peggy, *does he know?*

"First you must promise you won't say a word to anyone, not even to your Mama or Papa. Is that clear?"

"Yeah, whatever you say," he laughed as if there was nothing serious about Peggy's predicament.

"This is no joking matter. You think it's nothing, don't you?"

"Oh alright, I won't joke. Just tell me," he said while trying to look concerned.

"I was the one who cut the *Flora M* adrift."

"You what?" shouted James.

"Shush! You said you wouldn't tell."

James stood silent, disbelieving his ears.

"What got into your head? Why on earth would you do that?"

Peggy gave the full story with all the details about the Knottys, their plans, and how she had tried to intervene. When she finished, there was no smile on James' face. He was in a state of shock.

"I had no idea you were in such a mess. What were you thinking?"

"I had to stop those Knottys. Rosa doesn't want to go with them. There's no telling what they'll do. Especially now! Will you help me?"

"Of course," said James, "but how? There's a lot at stake, and I don't have the answer off the top of my head. It's going to take some kind of genius to figure this one out. I'll work on it on my way home."

"I'll be here for a while if you have any ideas."

As soon as James left, Billy came strutting out from behind his Pa's fish store. *Oh no! Not Billy again! Now what does he want?*

"Peggy, I'd like to have a word with you."

"Later Billy!"

"Later won't do. It has to be now! Why don't you co-operate just once?"

"Why should I? I have important things to do."

"I bet you do after last night," said Billy with a mischievous look. "Just give me two minutes."

"Fine! Two minutes, and no more," agreed Peggy in a nervous voice after Billy's comment.

"Last night, Pa was into the liquor, heavy. After

Rosa packed her stuff, she locked her bedroom door and wouldn't talk to anyone. I couldn't sleep so I went for a late walk and ended up at Pa's fish shed loft. That old hammock is pretty comfortable, so I crawled in, hoping to get some sleep. After a little nap, I woke up and strolled over to have a look out the window and guess what I saw?"

"Billy! Stop playing dumb. What do you want?"

"I want to know why."

"You asked me to help Rosa, didn't you?"

"That's a funny way to help."

"You should have been home in bed minding your own business."

"Rosa is my business. I was trying to come up with a plan to help her. Now why did you cut the *Flora M* adrift?"

"How do I know I can trust you?"

"I haven't said anything yet. You must have had a good reason for cutting that ship's anchor line, or were you just out rowing in your sleep?"

"You really bother me. How come you're always in my life when I don't want you nosing around? If you're really trying to help Rosa, I don't mind telling," and without waiting for Billy's answer, she asked, "Where on the *Flora M* is the Knottys' cabin?"

"At the stern of the ship, next to the Captain's. Why?"

"I have an idea. It just might come in handy. I cut the rope because I needed more time."

"For what?"

"To find out why they want Rosa. I think it has something to do with the fact that she looks like me. Maybe we can stop them from taking her."

"Impossible."

"Not if I have anything to do with it. All I need for you to do is stall the Knottys when they come to get Rosa. We don't have much time with the tide coming in. Who knows when they'll have *Flora M* afloat. Will you at least do that much?"

"Just leave it to me."

Billy hurried home, and sneaked to Rosa's door.

"It's me, Rosa."

"Come in," she whispered, and quickly closed the door behind him.

"Please help me," she begged while drying her eyes. "Pa won't listen. All my pleading hasn't changed his mind."

"I'm working on something. I need all the time I can get, so when the Knottys show up, keep them here as long as you can."

"What are you going to do?"

"I don't have time to explain, I gotta get out of here before Pa gets back."

"I'll do what I can. I just hope it works."

"Me too. I have to go."

No sooner had he spoken the words than Tom let out a bellow before coming inside the house.

"Billy! Get in here this minute!"

"Uh-oh! Too late," whispered Rosa. "Now what are we going to do?"

"Shh! I'm going out the window."

Rosa watched Billy escape and run zigzag behind every object that would hide him from his Pa. Tears began streaming down Rosa's face as she watched her brother flee.

Barely visible through the fog, practically every rowboat in the Cove was tied to the *Flora M*. The young boys and men rowed for all they were worth, hollering out the 'heave ho's to keep the pulling in unison.

Peggy watched anxiously. All too soon, the *Flora M* was safely pulled to deeper water and then anchored. The men returned to their work on the wharves.

Soon after, to Peggy's dismay, she saw the Knottys, the Captain, and a couple of crewmembers coming ashore. This would be her only chance. Panic sent her pacing.

"Why isn't Billy doing something so I can get out of

here?" she muttered. "He better hurry up, and not let me down!"

Billy knew of only one way to give Peggy the diversion she needed. He searched for a strong pole with which to carry out his plan. Then he snuck to old Susie's little home with its nearby outhouse. It was a tricky job trying to hide from his Pa and Susie at the same time. He couldn't help congratulating himself on his brilliant plan. *When I'm done, Susie will have the whole Cove stirred up like a swarm of hornets. This'll be the first time she'll want anyone around her place.*

By now he was within range. Ducking behind a boulder, he surveyed the landscape for any sign of life. The coast was clear. He started to make his move, but stopped short. Susie stepped outside with her broom in hand, making her way to the old lopsided outhouse. A couple of crows gawked and cawed at her.

"Get out of here you miserable crows! You're not gettin' nothin' from me!" she scowled while waving her broom. The crows flew off. Susie entered the outhouse, closed the door and latched it shut.

Of all the lousy rotten luck, thought Billy. *Now what'll I do?* He waited, and waited, and waited. *What's she doing in there anyway?* He knew Peggy was running out of time because he had spotted the Knottys coming ashore, too. His nerves were shaky and his patience ran out.

That's it! I can't wait another minute, he reasoned, and crept toward the outhouse with the pole in one hand and the biggest rock he could carry in the other.

Quickly and silently, he laid the rock close to the front of the outhouse, placed the pole between the rock and the sill, and then leaned on the end of the pole. Slowly, the creaking outhouse listed beyond the point of no return. Billy ran, heaving the pole into a pile of bushes to hide the evidence. Screams, threats, and broom thumping bellowed from the declining outhouse.

In no time, Billy was down over the bank, racing along the shore. It was a long way around, but nobody would see him as he headed for the point. From there he could see what was happening aboard the *Flora M.*

Down at the Cove, one of the fishermen held up his hands and said, "Listen! Who's that yelling?"

Everyone stopped their chatter and listened. They all looked in the direction of the upheaval.

"Susie's outhouse has fallen over and she's in it. Come on men, let's rescue Susie!" yelled John to everyone gathered around.

The surprised expressions on the men were one thing, but the hilarious giggles and laughter from the kids was something else. Like an army of ants, the throng rushed toward Susie's.

Peggy was thunderstruck at the drastic measure that Billy dared to carry out. Of course practically every woman heard John's alarm and those that didn't weren't long joining the throng to find out what all the commotion was about.

"This certainly is an exciting day at the Cove," commented John. "First the *Flora M* aground and now Susie's adrift in her outhouse."

Billy traveled off in the distance before sticking his head over the cliff to see what was happening. His idea worked beyond even his wildest dreams. By now, basically every soul in the Cove had gathered at Susie's outhouse. Folks were puzzled over the second mystery of the day and, as they assessed the predicament, everyone gave their opinion on solving the problem. Of course, Susie didn't let up with her threats and comments, which only added humor to the state of affairs. The buzz of comments silenced and anticipation grew on every face when the men dug in to rescue Susie from this stinky situation.

As Billy watched, he thought, *Peggy owes me for this one.*

With all the attention on Susie, nobody but Hector noticed Peggy as she slipped into the punt and rowed out to the *Flora M.* She had to admit, Billy did a fine job of clearing the Cove. She hoped nobody would find out that he did it, and why, or they'd both be in serious trouble.

Reaching the *Flora M*, Peggy gently climbed the ladder, and peeked over the rail to see if the deck was clear. Two seamen were stretched out and appeared to be sleeping, no doubt taking a rest after working hard to free the *Flora M.* Peggy climbed aboard, treading softly, and hid behind objects as she made her way to the Knottys' cabin. Before getting inside, she heard someone coming. Quickly she ducked behind a water barrel, and not a second too soon. She remained silent; a big man stopped, took a dipper, and had a long refreshing drink. Peggy could have touched his giant foot. He went into the Captain's quarters where three other men were playing cards. They were arguing that the dealer was cheating. The instant the big man went into the Captain's cabin, Peggy snuck into the Knottys' cabin.

When the Knottys arrived at the Robertson home, the agreement was finalized, and Tom accepted the money. The Knottys wanted to leave immediately in case Tom changed his mind.

"Come on Rosa, it's time to leave," Tom hollered.

With tears streaming down her face, Rosa came out of her room.

"Please Papa, don't make me go," she pleaded.

"Now enough of that! Remember, if you don't like it there, you can always come back. It's not like you haven't been away before."

"But I don't want to go!" she screamed.

"Mr. Knotty, would you and your wife mind stepping outside? I'd like to have a word with Rosa."

"Of course," they agreed and left.

Tom walked up to Rosa.

"If you so much as say another word about stayin', you'll be a sorry girl. Now get out that door, and keep your mouth shut. You go with those good people and appreciate the learnin' they're gonna give ya. I won't be so patient if you don't act like a proper lady. Now move!"

Rosa shuffled out the door to the Knottys. They made their way to the wharf, where their boat was tied up. This was the saddest day of Rosa's life.

Peggy had slipped into the Knotty's cabin, and began her search. She rooted through trunks, books, and any likely place to keep a portrait. She became frantic. Time was moving on. If she didn't find it soon, the Knottys would return.

Desperate, she threw off the bunk pillows. Her heart jumped. She stared with her eyes and mouth wide open. There was no question about it. That portrait was her, Hope MacEve. Joy and anxiety ran through her veins. She stood dazed and was so engrossed in her discovery; she lost all sense of time.

Before Peggy could decide what to do next, she heard the door fling open. She turned to see Mr. Knotty standing in the doorway, one hand clutching Rosa's suitcase while he stared dumbfounded at Peggy. Behind him was Rosa, streaming with tears, and the stern Mrs. Knotty. She stuck her pretty head over Mr. Knotty's shoulder, puzzled why he stopped. Surprise permeated the room. Mr. Knotty and Peggy glared at each other, both lost for words. Mrs. Knotty pushed Rosa aside, brushed past Oliver, and rushed toward Peggy, snatching the portrait from her hand.

"Why you impertinent sneaky little thief," snarled Mrs. Knotty.

Her scouring expression instantly changed to a devious smile.

"Well now, isn't this a stroke of luck," she exclaimed in a slow evil voice. "Look who decided to come with us Oliver."

Rosa remained frozen, until awakened to the fact that Mr. and Mrs. Knotty's attention was focused on Peggy. Quietly she slipped backwards out the door, hurried on deck, and raced for Peggy's punt. Frantically she untied the rope with her trembling hands. Suddenly a crewmember yelled, "Hey! Where do you think you're going? Get back here!"

Without hesitating, Rosa jumped onto the rail, held the rope tightly in her hand and leaped. She sailed through the air, over the punt, and into the blue with a huge splash. She began swimming before surfacing, pulling the boat behind her.

Mr. and Mrs. Knotty arrived on deck, dragging Peggy with them.

"Get her," ordered Mr. Knotty, pointing to Rosa.

"Never mind, Oliver. Let her go," interrupted Mrs. Knotty. "We don't need her, we have the real Hope. Captain, there's going to be a war. If you don't want to take on the whole village, I suggest you hasten to sail away from here."

Although they were already preparing to leave, the Captain gave the order to hustle. The crewmen scattered in all directions.

Peggy's eyes were glued on Rosa, who was now hanging onto the side of the punt. Would she be able to pull herself aboard, or would she have to swim to shore. Peggy held her breath as Rosa began bobbing up and down while holding onto the gunnels. On the third rise, to Peggy's surprise and delight, Rosa heaved herself into the punt, almost capsizing it as water spilled inside. She rolled over, hopped onto the seat, threw the oars in place, and rowed like a maniac.

Peggy watched, delighted with Rosa's success and wondered if she should bite Mrs. Knotty's arm, forcing her to let go. Could she run and jump just like Rosa? The thought of plunging into the deep terrified her. Then again, so did crossing the ocean. Facing a real storm would be worse than her nightmares. It was a tough decision, but before making her choice, the Knottys quickly ushered her below, and out of sight.

Billy had arrived at the point just in time to see Rosa sailing through the air. Her behavior shocked him, but not nearly as much as her frantic words the second she saw him.

"They got Peggy. Hurry! Do something," she yelled hysterically before reaching the shore.

"I'm thinking. I'm thinking."

"Well not fast enough! Look! They're leaving. They're kidnapping Peggy. Stop them!" screamed Rosa hysterically.

Billy paced, glaring between the *Flora M* and the Cove.

"Do something!" yelled Rosa.

"Quiet! Pa might be around and hear you! You go to Mary's and stay there. I'll find James and we'll go after Peggy. Now move!" he ordered and took off running.

Earlier, he had seen James heading toward his favourite spot, the dancing rock. He knew that's where James went whenever he needed to think. Billy leaped over crevices, jagged rocks, and boulders, yelling, "James! James!" Although it took only a minute, it seemed like an hour before he found him.

"They got Peggy," he yelled.

They raced back to the point, jumped into the punt, each grabbing an oar. Their speed would have made Rosa's rowing look like she was standing still.

"We can't lose sight of the *Flora M* or we'll never find her," warned Billy.

Hector was circling overhead, squealing and squawking.

"Dive-bomb them Hector. Slow them down!" yelled Billy, still out of breath.

"Winkle, get ready to sail!" shouted James half way to the *Senora* .

"What's wrong?" he asked.

"They kidnapped Peggy. We're going after her!"

Chapter 6
Peggy's Capture

Back in their quarters, Mrs. Knotty laid down the law. "Now you listen, and listen well," she snapped at Peggy. "Let's get one thing straight from the start. If anyone asks what connection you have with us, tell them you are our adopted daughter. Is that clear?"

"It's clear, but not true."

Mrs. Knotty replied, "We have adoption papers that prove we are your guardians. That's all you need to know."

Yeah! Phony ones, thought Peggy.

"And one more thing," warned Mrs. Knotty while she dug her fingers into Peggy's shoulders and glared into her eyes. "If you say you are *anything* other than our adopted daughter, there will be severe consequences. Our associates in Aberdeen will visit the Cove for unpleasant reasons if anything goes wrong. Finally, you are to remain by our side no matter what. Do you understand or do I need to spell it out in no uncertain terms?"

"I understand your threat, Mrs. Knotty."

"Well, now that we have this matter cleared up, let's enjoy our trip," she said with a smile.

As the days wore on, Mr. Knotty often took Peggy on deck while Mrs. Knotty bathed and prettied herself up. One clear morning as they walked past the helmsman Peggy asked politely, "May I look through the telescope, sir?"

"I suppose so, but you'd better be careful. Drop it and the Captain will feed you to the sharks," he replied with a grin.

"Thank you, sir. I will be very careful. I would hate to be eaten by a shark. The thought gives me the shivers."

Peggy turned to face the bow and searched. She asked Mr. Knotty, "Is that a pirate ship ahead?"

"Let me have a look," he said, and raised the telescope. "No and lucky for you. They'd force you to be their cook and you'd never be free again. Do you agree?"

"I'd put something in their food to make them all sick. Then I'd escape."

"No doubt you would," he laughed, intrigued by Peggy's wit and intelligence. He concluded she would make a fine lawyer, but that was out of the question. Secretly, once or twice, the idea of having a daughter of his own touched his heart. Hannah would wring his neck if she knew he even thought such a thing, so he quickly erased his foolish notion.

Mr. Knotty handed the telescope back to Peggy and she searched the horizon behind them. Sails, way off in the distance, were too small to identify. She had seen only a few ships thus far.

During their journey, Peggy was watching for more than ships. She studied the Knottys' behavior; she knew they kept a close eye on her too. Mrs. Knotty became suspicious.

"Oliver, I'm warning you, that girl is up to something and you're getting a little too chummy with her. She isn't as upset as one would expect."

"There you go again, jumping to conclusions. I wouldn't dare let her jeopardize our plans. I wish you would find something good to say about me once in a while."

Oliver knew Hannah was right, because Peggy had a charm that wiggled its way into a tiny piece of his cold heart. He'd be doomed if he admitted it.

Drawings by Brandon Fraser

During their voyage, some days brought pouring rain and, at times, not enough wind. Peggy asked Mrs. Knotty for paper and ink to pass the time by drawing. She drew lots of her favourite critters with big eyes and happy faces that helped cheer her up. It gave her practice before attempting a portrait of Mrs. Knotty, who was quite flattered by the stunning resemblance. Even Peggy was surprised how well it turned out and thought it made Mrs. Knotty more beautiful than she really was. Mrs. Knotty's comment set Peggy back on her heels.

"Why that looks almost as perfect as I am, maybe you'll do better the next time," she boasted.

While crossing the Atlantic, Peggy's biggest obstacle was her fear of another storm. Then one night it happened. She fell asleep during a steady breeze, but later, broadside gale force winds and heavy seas caused the ship to list more than usual. A huge wave tipped the boat over so far that it dumped Peggy from her bunk. She landed beside Mrs. Knotty. Unfortunately, during her fall, her elbow collided directly into Mrs. Knotty's nose. She let out a piercing scream and rolled around while holding her nose.

"Oooh! My nose, my nose! It's bleeding. Oliver! Light the lamp, and get this clumsy thing off me!" she ordered.

Mr. Knotty stumbled about in the tossing ship. "Hurry up you lumbering idiot before I bleed to death."

"If you're so smart, why don't you light the lamp yourself?" he fired back.

"Because I can't hold my handkerchief and strike a match at the same time. If I had three hands, I'd show you!"

Mr. Knotty said no more and after a few more attempts, succeeded in lighting the lamp.

With the ship being tossed about, Peggy couldn't hide her fear. She trembled, her teeth chattered, and terror raged in her eyes. Mr. Knotty looked at Peggy with sympathy.

"If you're cold, Peggy, there are more blankets," he offered.

"She's not cold Oliver! Can't you see she's terrified?" barked Mrs. Knotty, still annoyed at Peggy's tumble.

Although the seas were rough, Mrs. Knotty didn't believe the ship would sink. Her confidence provided an opportunity to torture Peggy by instilling more fear into her heart.

"If this storm doesn't let up soon, we'll all drown," she exclaimed, while pretending she was gasping for air.

"Don't make it sound worse than it is Hannah," scolded Mr. Knotty.

"Don't interfere, Oliver!" she warned, pointing her finger at him.

Quickly, she turned, placing her smug face only inches from Peggy's.

"Tonight you are going to diiiie," she drawled with a hideous laugh.

In a flash, she glared at Mr. Knotty.

"Unless that sympathetic look is for my battered nose, wipe it off your face this instant."

"I think that's quite enough, Hannah. Let's try to get a little more sleep."

"Enough? Sleep? Do you think I'll be able to sleep with this throbbing pain? If my nose is broken, you'll pay dearly young lady. Now, the both of you get back in your bunks before I loose my temper. I don't want to see or hear from either of you before morning!"

Those aboard the *Senora* had their own problems to deal with during the storm. James was concerned about breaking a mast with the amount of sail that was up and asked Winkle and Billy to reef them.

"If we reef the sails, we won't be able to keep up to the *Flora M*," warned Winkle.

"I know, but it's better than breaking a mast. Besides, we lost sight of the *Flora M* long ago."

"Are you telling me we came all this way, only to lose them?" shouted Billy. "How'll we find Peggy?"

"I'm hoping they'll still be in sight when this storm passes. We better tie a lifeline to ourselves; I don't want anyone lost if we're washed overboard. Those waves are getting too big for comfort."

"Too bad the *Senora* wasn't bigger!" shouted Billy. "Are we going to be alright?" he asked with concern.

"I've been in bad storms with Captain Simms," answered Winkle. "But if this gets any worse, it'll be more than we bargained for."

"What if we can't find the *Flora M* tomorrow?" asked Billy, still not convinced.

"From the course they are taking and what you heard the Knottys say to your Pa, I'm sure they're heading for Aberdeen," assured James.

"I wish I'da asked for their address before I left," fumed Billy.

"We'll find them Billy, don't worry. Right, Winkle?"

"He's right, Billy, James is like an old bloodhound. He'll find them."

Back on the *Flora M*, Peggy didn't sleep another wink the rest of the night. She was relieved the next day when, by noon, the stormy weather had subsided. But there was still a storm raging in Mrs. Knotty's heart.

"I should give you a good bash across the nose so you'll know how it feels," she threatened Peggy. "Just look how swollen and bruised mine is," she complained.

"Mrs. Knotty, I couldn't help falling out of my bunk. I was asleep. I'm sorry it happened, but it wasn't like I planned it," defended Peggy.

"Peggy's right, Hannah! It was an accident," agreed Mr. Knotty.

"Oliver! From now on, tie her in that bunk. I won't stand for another bash."

"I'll have the carpenter put a higher board on the edge of her bunk. That'll be sufficient."

"It better be or you'll pay too."

Fortunately, Mrs. Knotty's nose wasn't broken, and the swelling subsided within a few days.

After the storm, James caught up to the *Flora M* by staying on course. The *Senora* was more capable of pointing, which enabled James to overtake the *Flora M* before reaching their destination. At Aberdeen Harbour, they tied up the *Senora* and nestled her between larger ships to keep her camouflaged, but still offer a decent view of the ships coming and going through the harbour.

Peggy tried to melt Mrs. Knotty's heart, but her efforts failed to warm their cold relationship. As they neared their journey's end, Peggy overheard Mrs. Knotty speaking.

"Oliver, tonight we must discuss how we are going to deal with Peggy and Judge Sampson."

"Yes, I was planning to speak to you about that as well," agreed Mr. Knotty.

Chapter 7
Reaching Scotland

As the *Flora M* entered Aberdeen Harbour, Peggy's heart fluttered. She concentrated on the landscape around the harbour. Something familiar about the long breakwater triggered a memory. She hoped her mind would crack wide open, illuminating the past. *It's the lighthouse. I'm sure it's the one I saw when we left Aberdeen. People were lined up along the breakwater, waving as we sailed past. Was it real or did I dream it?* She wondered.

While in this quiet blissful state, Mrs. Knotty soured Peggy's sweet moment when she demanded with sarcasm, "Why are you looking so joyful?"

"I'm happy because we made it here safely and I believe I'll soon remember everything as clear as the noonday sun. You know how bright and glorious it is after being hidden by thick fog for weeks? Well try to imagine my mind! It's like I've been in the fog for years. You'd be happy, too! Right?"

"The only thing you need to remember and be clear about is how to behave and be quiet. Never mind trying to dig up the past. You have the future to worry about."

I bet I do, Peggy reasoned.

Beforehand, James, Billy, and Winkle had rehearsed their plan to perfection. They waited, hoping their calculations were correct. Finally they heard the words

that were like music to their ears: "There she is, boys, the
Flora M," announced Winkle, as he lowered the telescope.
"Are you ready for an adventure?"

"You mean chasing those Knottys across the Atlantic
wasn't an adventure?" questioned Billy.

James and Winkle laughed.

"Not like the one we're about set out on. This is going
to be a first hand experience, Billy. Let's see how good you
are as a detective," said Winkle. "We better hurry if we
want to be ready when the Knottys come ashore."

Still aboard the *Flora M*, the Knottys were preparing to
visit Judge Sampson. Mrs. Knotty warned Peggy to be on
her best behavior and not to pull any heroic stunts. "You
keep your comments to yourself and never mind asking
questions. Be seen and not heard. Remember, if anything
goes wrong, our friends will be visiting the Cove. Do I
make myself clear?" threatened Mrs. Knotty.

"Yes, ma'am! I'll be as good as gold. I'm so excited. If you
tell me everything, I won't have to ask one question, right?"

"There you go again! Now, I mean it! Mr. Knotty and
I have important matters to deal with. That is my
last warning!"

"I don't understand why you can't tell me about my
homeland. Nobody's visiting with you now," replied Peggy
putting in her most convincing voice. "I thought you would
at least give the Judge the idea that you cared for me."

"We'll take care of the loving after we get this business
put to rest," promised Mrs. Knotty.

That's what I'm afraid of, thought Peggy.

After gathering their belongings, the three walked off
the *Flora M*. Mr. Knotty was in front, Peggy next, followed
by Mrs. Knotty. Peggy came to the end of the gangplank.

Winkle brushed between Peggy and Mrs. Knotty,
almost knocking her to the ground. "Excuse me. My
humble apologies, madam," assured Winkle, as he reached
out to help steady her from falling.

The instant Winkle distracted Mrs. Knotty, James and Billy quickly stepped in, each grabbing one of Peggy's hands. "Don't say a word, just come with us," ordered James in a low voice, as he and Billy half dragged Peggy into the crowd and away from the Knottys. She was dumbfounded, happy and excited to see James. She gave him a quick hug, but was annoyed at the sight of Billy. "What's he doing here?"

"We're taking you home. Hurry!" said Billy with a big smile. That's when they heard Mrs. Knotty calling Hope's name.

"Let's go," said Billy, and latched onto Peggy, trying to run. He came to a sudden halt when she didn't budge.

"Stop it! You're ruining everything!" exclaimed Peggy as she pushed Billy's hand away.

Billy and James were totally confused. "What are you talking about?" insisted James.

"I'm trying to find my family. The Knottys are my only chance. We're on our way to Judge Sampson's."

"You're crazy!" said Billy, shaking his head.

Mrs. Knotty was getting closer. "Hope! Hope! Where are you?" she shouted frantically.

"We have to get out of here," insisted Billy.

"No! I'm not leaving!" resolved Peggy, but before she knew it, Billy scooped her in his arms, threw her on his shoulder like a sack of potatoes, and ran.

James, taken by surprise, meant to run after them, but tripped while trying to dodge a lady who had her arms full with a set of twins, and three older children following behind her.

"Put me down!" yelled Peggy while kicking, and pounding Billy on his back.

"Not on your life. We didn't chase you across the Atlantic for nothing!" he answered while racing through the crowd.

"Let me go or you'll be sorry," warned Peggy.

"That'll be the day. You're in no position to stop me

now!" he laughed. "I never thought I'd enjoy having you near me, but this is hilarious."

"That's what you think! See if this is hilarious!" retorted Peggy as she remembered what John did the day he got into his fight with that fellow who kept pinging his ear. Instantly Peggy slipped off Billy's suspenders.

"Stop that," he yelled. But it was too late. His pants slipped down past his knees, which sent him flying, forcing him to let go of Peggy or smash his face into the stony road.

"I warned you," she said, and disappeared, while Billy struggled to conceal his embarrassment.

Mrs. Knotty was still calling Hope's name in a frenzy. Peggy, annoyed with Mrs. Knotty's inconsideration by refusing to call her Peggy, wouldn't answer. Finally Mr. Knotty called out, "Peggy! Peggy! I'm over here. Can you hear me?"

Peggy answered, "Yes," while weaving through the crowd toward Mr. Knotty.

"What happened?" asked Mr. Knotty, in a panic as Peggy ran to his side.

"Two young men grabbed me and tried to take me away!" gasped Peggy, all out of breath. "I tricked them and got away. It's a good thing you were calling Mr. Knotty. I knew exactly where to find you."

"And I suppose you couldn't hear me?" scolded Mrs. Knotty.

"I heard someone calling, but it wasn't for Peggy."

"You knew very well I was calling you," scorned Mrs. Knotty.

"Never mind, you two. Peggy, watch out for any more hoodlums!" wheezed Mr. Knotty. "You better hold onto my hand," he said as he flagged a carriage. They climbed inside, and began their journey to visit Judge Sampson. "Take us to 666 McJustice Road," instructed Mr. Knotty. "And please hurry!"

Winkle and James had tracked Billy down, who by now had regained his dignity. All three were stunned by

Peggy's wild scheme. "You go back and stay on the *Senora*, Winkle. Billy and I will grab a carriage and hopefully find the Knottys."

"Look, there's Mrs. Knotty in the carriage that's going around the corner. I'd recognize that hat anywhere. We better hurry," urged Billy. "Peggy said something about going to see Judge Sampson."

"Come on, Billy. Maybe the drivers will know where the Judge's office is," insisted James as he ran toward a number of carriages lined up at the dock. They pushed through the crowd, trying to find a carriage that wasn't occupied.

"Over there, James. That one doesn't have anyone in it," shouted Billy as they shoved their way to the driver.

"Do you know where Judge Sampson's office is?" asked James.

"Yes, sir. Every driver in Aberdeen knows that."

"Good, will you take us there?" asked Billy before James spoke.

"Sorry, I'm waiting for someone."

"Now what, James? We have to get there right away."

"If you're in a hurry, try further down along the dock. There's a ship leaving in a few hours. No doubt you'll find a driver looking for business after dropping off his passengers."

"Thanks," said James as he and Billy ran to find the ship.

Pushing and dodging through the activity along the dock slowed their progress, but at last they arrived at the ship, but not one carriage was in sight. "Come on, somebody show up," urged Billy as he walked around trying to calm his nerves.

"We can't wait any longer Billy. Let's ask directions to Judge Sampson's and go on foot."

Billy agreed and they darted off. Billy took one last look back at the ship before heading up the street. Still no carriages. They didn't get far when a carriage, loaded with people rode out from a side street. "Ask that driver," shouted Billy.

"Excuse me sir! Would you please tell us how to get to Judge Sampson's office?" asked James.

"I can do better than that. I can take you there just as soon as I drop off my passengers at the ship that's around the corner."

"Great! We'll meet you there," said James as they ran back to the ship.

"Do you mind if we help unload?" asked James, "We have an emergency!"

"Give us a hand then," said the gentleman as he paid the driver.

Billy and James unloaded the luggage, jumped into the carriage, and the driver rode off. When they turned onto the Judge's street, James warned the driver, "We must not be seen. Please stop far enough away to be inconspicuous."

"Yes sir, that's easy," said the driver, and he stopped.

In the carriage, while on their way to Judge Sampson's office, Peggy memorized every building and street she could cram into her brain. She wanted to know how to get back to the *Senora* in case she had to flee. Before too long, they arrived outside the Judge's office. Mrs. Knotty gave Peggy a final threat to follow her instructions as outlined earlier.

As they stepped out of the carriage, Mr. Knotty warned, "Remember Hannah, this is strictly business."

"Relax Oliver, if I had wanted Frank, I would have had him."

"Mrs. Knotty, were you and Judge Sampson sweethearts at one time?" asked Peggy.

For once Mrs. Knotty didn't bark at Peggy for asking a question, but smiled with her head held high, looking straight ahead.

"You might say that," she said confidently.

"Never mind thinking about the Judge, Hannah. You make sure you back me up and keep the facts straight about Peggy," he warned as he opened the door of the building where Judge Sampson's office was located.

"Oliver, you do your part and I'll do mine," she whispered to him while he closed the door behind them. Down the hall, and above another door, a brass sign with black letters read, 'Judge F. Sampson.'

As they approached Judge Sampson's office, Peggy was amused at Mr. Knotty's jealously. She watched with interest as they entered. The young lady at the desk greeted them and said, "Please be seated, I'll notify Judge Sampson that you have arrived."

"Thank you ma'am," replied Mr. Knotty, who was obviously nervous.

The secretary knocked as she entered the Judge's office, partially closing the door after stepping inside. She came out a few seconds later.

"Judge Sampson will be with you momentarily," she said.

Before meeting the Knottys, the Judge looked in the mirror, combed his hair, and made sure his appearance was in perfect order. Seconds later he walked briskly from his office to the reception area.

"Well, well. How good to see you again, Hannah. It's been a long time," greeted the Judge as he shook her hand, totally ignoring Mr. Knotty.

"Yes, and thanks to your generous offer, we meet again," she replied with a pleasant smile.

"You are most welcome," assured Judge Sampson while he continued holding her hand and staring into her eyes.

Mr. Knotty, indignant over their behavior, cleared his throat to let Hannah know she had crossed the line, and he stepped in to break the Judge's spell.

"Judge Sampson, we are here on business. This is not a social call, so please; let's get this over with. As you can see we have been successful in locating Hope MacEve," he said sternly as he held the portrait of Peggy for the Judge to confirm her identity.

"My apologies, Mr. Knotty, I was unaware you were in

such a hurry. Let me see now," he smiled as he looked at Peggy.

"Are you Hope MacEve?"

"If that is my portrait I am, but I haven't been able to remember a thing before the shipwreck. All I know is I'm Peggy. The Knottys tell me I'm Hope MacEve. What do you think?"

"By the look of you, I believe you are Hope. I briefly met your Mama and Papa on several occasions. Once you came to my office with him. You have your Mama's features. No doubt you are Hope MacEve. I'm sorry to learn of your misfortune. Your Papa and Mama were highly regarded from what little I knew of them."

Peggy's eyes became moist, thrilled to know she looked like her Mama. Her heart lightened. A connection, she now had an idea of her Mama's looks. She was still curious about her Papa.

"My Papa, do I look anything like him?" she asked eagerly.

The Judge studied her carefully.

"I'd say you have his chin. That's about it, from what I recall."

Peggy remained silent, looking off into the distance.

"Well young lady, you have an inheritance. Apparently, there is a chest at Castle Fraise. It has the name F. MacEve on top. Good luck."

Peggy hardly heard a word after discovering she strongly resembled her Mama. She was so absorbed in her thoughts that nothing else mattered.

The Judge brought her back to reality when he said, "There is something else," and handed Peggy the poem.

Peggy beamed as she unfolded the paper and looked at the words written by her Papa. The handwriting was clearly legible. She began to read it immediately. Her expression caused the Judge to smile.

"Strange thing to give a child isn't it. I hope you like it," he said, while shaking his head.

"I don't understand what your Papa saw in that. Perhaps someday you'll figure it out."

"Thank you Judge," said Peggy.

The puzzled look on Peggy's face aroused the Knottys' curiosity.

"What does it say?" asked Mrs. Knotty as she and Mr. Knotty leaned forward, trying to read the words.

"It talks about her venture through life," said the Judge.

"Read it to us," encouraged Mrs. Knotty.

Peggy read the first two lines, but when Mrs. Knotty heard 'Aim for the highest goals,' in the third line, she interrupted. "That's enough. I don't need anyone telling me what to welcome or what to aim for."

"Those are good things, Mrs. Knotty. Don't you agree, Judge Sampson?" asked Peggy.

The Judge chuckled.

"We can't deny that, but I think Mrs. Knotty understands all that."

"Judge Sampson, is there anything else we need to know, or are we finished?" asked the impatient Mr. Knotty.

"Nothing but settling the payment for your work, Mr. Knotty," said Judge Sampson. "Perhaps Mrs. Knotty and Peggy could wait outside."

"Come along, child," ordered Mrs. Knotty, "We must leave at once."

Mrs. Knotty's cold voice shattered Peggy's pleasurable

moments thinking about her Mama and Papa. In a whirl, Peggy's thoughts focused on the present and she began putting the pieces together. She now understood the Knottys' devious plans to snatch her inheritance. *So that's why they wanted Rosa. They were going to pretend she was Hope MacEve, to fool the judge. And Mrs. Knotty thinks I'm sneaky!*

Peggy felt alone and trapped, and wished she had at least let James and Billy follow without being noticed by the Knottys.

When James and Billy arrived at Judge Sampson's, they were happy to see the carriage that the Knottys had hired. In less than half a minute, Mrs. Knotty and Peggy walked out of the building and stepped into the carriage.

"There they are!" said Billy as he nudged James with his elbow.

Billy was getting impatient.

"I wish we knew what they were up to. I hate this guessing game," he protested.

James had noticed the street kids hustling the carriages for opportunities to carry bags to earn a few coins. There was a little fellow hanging around their carriage.

"Young man, how'd you like an important job? We'll pay you handsomely," whispered James as the boy walked by.

"Yes sir! I'm your man," agreed the boy.

"It's a secret mission."

"I wouldn't squeal to save my life."

"Good!" agreed Billy. "Hire him, James."

"It's very easy, here's all you have to do," instructed James as he gave the details. The lad set off with a merry heart, confident in his ability to fulfill the task.

Shortly thereafter Mr. Knotty arrived and attempted to step into the coach, but before he could be seated he was suddenly yanked to a halt. A strange man pulled on his coattails. He reminded Peggy of a bulldog.

"Not so fast, Barrister! Three days, eh? More like three months," said the stranger.

Mr. Knotty slightly turned his head while speaking.

"I was urgently called overseas on business and just returned today as a matter of fact. You tell Mr. Betts I have very good news. I'll contact him in a day or two."

"Hand over the money now or we'll be taking a trip to Mr. Betts' warehouse."

Oliver knew all too well what that meant. It was now or never. With one swift kick to the stomach, Oliver sent the goon rolling backward to the ground.

"Go driver!" ordered Mr. Knotty. "Take us to Castle Fraise."

Mr. Betts' goon smiled as he beat off the dust and straightened his clothes. "Castle Fraise, aye."

The boy had also heard Mr. Knotty instructing the driver. He ran to James and Billy with the good news.

"They're going to Castle Fraise," he told them.

"Good job my friend. Here's your reward," said James.

"Wow! Thank you sir. I'm at your service any time."

"You're welcome. Driver, do you know where Castle Fraise is?"

"Certainly. About sixteen miles from here."

"Will you take us there?"

"Yes sir!" He cracked the whip as they darted off.

"We must stay back, and out of sight from Barrister Knotty," instructed James.

"No problem, I'll stop for a couple of minutes to feed and water my horse. That should put enough distance between us.

Mr. Knotty's encounter with the goon sent Mrs. Knotty into another rage. She started interrogating him about the incident.

"Oliver! What are you hiding from me?" she demanded with a stern look.

"I will not discuss our personal affairs in front of Peggy."

"You mean Hope," interrupted Mrs. Knotty.

"I don't remember being Hope," said Peggy. "Please call me Peggy."

"We'll call you what we want. You just mind your manners, young lady," snarled Mrs. Knotty.

Peggy knew it was in her best interest to keep silent, so she concentrated on memorizing every new sight. The countryside overwhelmed her and reminded her of Fraser's Hill back at Janet's. Numerous shades of green covered the hills, fields, and trees. She knew she had been here before. The winding road exhilarated her hopes, and when they crossed the bridge over the River Don, she was reminded of the one at Wooden's River.

It was a tense ride to the Castle. Mr. Knotty had to get that money fast. It was his only chance that Mr. Betts might spare his neck.

Chapter 8
Castle Fraise Mysteries

As Castle Fraise came into view, Peggy couldn't sit still because of her anticipation.

"Oh, isn't it beautiful? Surely, something will come back to me. Isn't this exciting?"

"You have no idea how exciting it is," assured Mrs. Knotty.

"I'll second that," agreed Mr. Knotty. "Driver, please take the carriage around back."

After leaving the carriage, Mr. Knotty led the way as they walked to the main entrance of the castle and knocked. Moments later, the large wooden door slowly opened.

"May I help you?" politely asked the butler.

"Yes sir. I'm Barrister Knotty, and I would like to speak with Colonel MacEve please."

"Aye! Barrister Knotty. I'm afraid the Colonel is away at the moment. However, Judge Sampson had informed him some time ago that you had been sent overseas in search of Hope. Colonel MacEve thought you might be arriving soon. He instructed me to allow you access to the castle if you happened to return while he was away."

"Thank you. That is most generous. Well, we'll try to complete our business quickly," he said in a nervous tone. "Do you have a quiet place that we can use as an office?"

"Why yes, Mr. Knotty, the chapel is the ideal spot. Follow me."

Peggy was awed while climbing the spiral stairs to the chapel. It was so thrilling. She looked in every direction, trying to find something to remind her of her past. She thought about the chest and what was in it. Her joy turned to anxiety, knowing the Knottys planned to steal her inheritance, and the threat to harm Mary or her family if she exposed their plans.

"Here we are," said the butler. "Now make yourselves comfortable. I must remind you Mr. Knotty, nothing is to be removed before Colonel MacEve returns."

"Of course. Thank you for your help."

As Billy and James approached the castle, they were apprehensive.

"There's no sign of the Knottys, I hope we've beaten them here," said James.

"We won't be long finding out," figured Billy.

They hurried to the main entrance and knocked. Soon the butler answered the door.

"Yes, may I help you?" he intoned rather coldly at the sight of Billy and James.

"It's urgent that we speak to Mr. MacEve," insisted James.

"To whom am I speaking?" asked the butler.

"I'm James and this is Billy. My family took care of Peggy, I mean Hope, when she was shipwrecked."

"I'm sorry, but you're too late. Colonel MacEve is away."

"Is there any way we can contact him? It's important. We're afraid Peggy is in danger with Barrister and Mrs. Knotty," stressed James.

"Miss Hope, in danger with Barrister and Mrs. Knotty! Preposterous!" said the butler.

"Barrister Knotty and his wife kidnapped Peggy. We don't know what they are up to, but we must speak to her," pressed Billy.

"Kidnapped! Nonsense. Now you two be on your way, and find something useful to do," warned the butler as he began closing the door.

"But sir..." continued James, to no avail. They were shut out.

"Now what?" asked Billy, who was severely frustrated.

"We have to find a way into the castle," persisted James.

"Yeah? And how? Climb the walls? And what are we going to do even if we do get inside?"

"I'm not sure, but I sense Peggy is going to need us. There must be a window or door we can sneak through. I'm going around back. Are you coming Billy, or do I have to go alone?"

"I'm coming, keep close to the walls so they won't see us from inside."

Around back, about mid-way around the castle, two large bushes nestled beside the servants' entrance offered a good hiding place. Billy and James darted for the bushes and waited. Two servants left the castle and entered the nearby stable.

"That door isn't locked, let's go inside," insisted James.

"What if someone sees us?"

"We'll tell them the truth, that we're friends of Peggy and that she could be in danger."

"And you think they'll believe us?"

"Do you have a better plan?" asked James.

"Yeah! Tell them we are the new stable boys."

"No. We'll stick to the truth, now let's go."

Inside, along the hallway, a number of doors appeared to be the servant's quarters. The third door was ajar.

"Maybe nobody's there. James, you check down the hall. I'll try this door that's ajar," whispered Billy.

He peeked through the crack of the opened door. Two servant girls were inside, packing the last of their goodies into a large picnic basket. Billy silently darted off, tapping James on the shoulder and motioning to him about the danger. Without hesitating they both slipped inside another room just as the two girls left.

"That was too close," sighed Billy.

James didn't answer. He was too busy grabbing an outfit that hung behind the door.

"What are you doing?" asked Billy.

"You'll see, follow me."

James opened the door a crack; then stuck his head out to see if anyone was in sight.

"Come on Billy. The coast is clear."

James rushed to the room that the two girls had just left. "In here," he said to Billy, and began rummaging around.

"Now what?" asked Billy.

"Here!" whispered James as he threw a uniform to Billy. "Hurry up and put that on."

Billy glared at the uniform; he was mortified. He held it up to confirm his suspicion, and immediately shoved it back in James' face.

"You're crazy if you think I'm wearing that!"

"Get it on, and fast before someone finds us."

"I wouldn't be caught dead in a dress. You wear it, I'm not!" protested Billy.

"I'd make a strange looking woman with whiskers."

"Well I'm not dressin' in no woman's clothes. So there," persisted Billy.

"You have no choice. Now move it," warned James as he went to the bureau and found the undergarments for the ladies outfit. "Peggy helped Rosa, now it's your turn to help Peggy."

"You'll pay for this," threatened Billy while he rolled up his pant legs before pulling the pantaloons over them. Billy had never tried to put a dress on before and he was getting all tangled up in it, so James helped slip it over Billy's head. They stuffed the dress with rags to give him a full figured bosom, and finished off with spectacles and a bonnet to cover his hair.

"Put this on too," instructed James, handing Billy a bodice while he was dressing into the manservant's uniform.

"Get that out of here. I'm not wearing that thing."

"Aw, come on," coaxed James. "Remember you have to fool those Knottys."

"Not with that I don't. It's too frilly in the front."

"You don't want them to know you're a fake, do you?"

"Of course not."

"You'll be pretty close to them at times. This isn't a party we're going to. You'll probably never have another chance to outsmart the Knottys. You don't want them to recognize you."

"Oh alright, if that's what it takes. Man, how do women handle all this gear?" he fumed.

"Never mind," said James. "Help me look like an old man whose days are almost over."

"My pleasure," smiled Billy, who was looking for a little revenge. "Let me help. Close your eyes." He reached in the fireplace, grabbed some ashes, and rubbed them in James' hair.

James was about to leave, when Billy said, "Hold still, I'm not finished," and, with delight, smeared soot over James' face. He then added some rice powder and threw a cane in his hand.

"Now you look like an old man. You better put on a pair of gloves to cover those hands. With that, I think you'll not only fool the Knottys, but Peggy too," he said with satisfaction. "Now let's go."

James and Billy ran through the castle whenever nobody was in sight, but crept along as they entered a room, or turned a corner; just in case somebody might be there. They were desperate to find Peggy and the Knottys.

Back at the chapel, the Knottys were anxious to get on with their search for the trunk. The butler, who happened to be recently hired, was driving them beyond the point of impatience with his extensive chatter about the castle, but when he began relating facts about his own family, Mr. Knotty had enough.

"Thank you for your help sir, but we should be about our business if you don't mind."

"Oh I'm sorry, Mr. Knotty, I do get carried away with my talking. Please excuse me," he said, and left the chapel.

James and Billy halted as they entered the hall at the opposite end of the chapel. They waited for the butler to disappear. Mr. and Mrs. Knotty also waited for the butler to be out of sight.

"Shouldn't we take Peggy with us?" asked Oliver.

Mrs. Knotty took him aside and whispered, "I don't think she should see what's inside that chest."

"Clever idea," agreed Oliver, "but we can't just leave her here."

"That's true. You start looking elsewhere. I'll stay in this area to keep an eye on her. There's only one door to the chapel."

"Fine!" agreed Oliver, "but watch her closely."

"Oliver! Since when did you have to tell *me* what to do?" said Hannah, as she walked back to Peggy.

"Missy, you stay put while we take care of our business. Remember! One false move and we'll take care of your friends at the Cove!" warned Mrs. Knotty again as she quickly backed out of the door. Accidently she bumped into an elderly gentleman, almost knocking him to the floor. If it hadn't been for the maid holding his arm, no doubt he would have fallen.

"Watch where you're going, Hannah!" shouted Mr. Knotty.

"I'm terribly sorry," she apologized, and instantly turned up her nose at the smell of soot and ashes.

"Ya need eyes in the back uf yer head lass," said the old gentleman in a shaky voice, and waved his hand. "Don't cha wurry, I'm fine!" he said as they continued on their way.

Peggy placed her hands to cover her face so Mrs. Knotty wouldn't see her reaction. It was rather amusing to see Mrs. Knotty in the awkward position for a change.

Mrs. Knotty, wishing to avoid any further scolding, directed the attention to Oliver.

"Be off," she insisted.

"I will, but for heavens sake Hannah, be careful," scolded Mr. Knotty, while they watched the two staff continue their walk down the hall.

"My they have uncouth staff," whispered Mrs. Knotty,

glaring at maid's mannish walk. I wonder why they keep *them* here?"

"Hannah! Please! Mind your manners," pleaded Mr. Knotty as he left to begin his search.

Mrs. Knotty stuck her head through the chapel door, pointed her finger at Peggy, and warned, "Remember what I said!"

Now that the Knottys were gone, Peggy reached for the poem that she had tucked away in her dress pocket. Reading it would help pass the time and keep her from being bored. She wondered what the note said.

She casually read each line, thinking it was a strange poem that her Papa wrote. No wonder the Judge thought so, too.

However, the second time through she read it more carefully, studying each word, line, and verse. She tried visualizing the scenes it portrayed. The third time, she read hastily, and other times very slowly. The words that captured her attention the most were 'let every dream catch her.' Something was starting to become clear. The anticipation drove her to her feet. In her haste the poem accidentally slipped from her fingers. The moment she stooped to pick it up, a servant lady walked in and gasped, "Well hello Hope! I can't believe my eyes. You have no idea how shocked and pleased I was when the butler told me you were here."

Immediately Peggy knew she had heard that voice before, but where? She looked up, searching for a connection.

"I'm Miss Finney! Don't you remember?"

"Miss Finney! You're Miss Finney," repeated Peggy.

"Yes! You must remember how you and your Pa teased me! Poor..."

"Poor...Miss Finney," repeated Peggy.

"That's right! Go on. She met..."encouraged Miss Finney.

"She met...a man...so...skinny!"shouted Peggy. "When he... asked...her...hand in marriage, she left him in the carriage."

"That's it," laughed Miss Finney, rushing to embrace Peggy.

"Finally, somebody I know!" Peggy answered, as tears of joy trickled down her cheeks.

"Let me take a good look at you. My, how you've grown!" exclaimed Miss Finney as she stood back and gazed at Peggy in disbelief. She and Peggy were laughing and crying at the same time.

Abruptly, Miss Finney paused, "What do you mean, 'finally, someone I know'? Of course you know me! Where have you been? What has happened to you? How did you get here?"

"Oh, Miss Finney, so much has happened. Where do I begin?"

"Tell me everything!"

"I can't remember anything before the shipwreck. Now and then I have bits and pieces of the past, but you're the first person I can remember. That's why I'm so excited."

"We feared the worst when we didn't hear a word."

"I was the only survivor."

"I'm so sorry," Miss Finney sympathized, as she held Peggy, and gently stroked her long, beautiful hair. She had combed it on occasion when Peggy had visited Castle Fraise. "Go on."

After Peggy told Miss Finney everything that had happened since the shipwreck, she wanted to know all about her Mama and Papa.

"You mean to say you can't remember them either?"

"That's right. Nothing."

"That's terrible. I find this so hard to believe."

"I know, but it's true. Now, please, tell me."

"Oh, Mr. MacEve was a happy go lucky man, always teasing us with riddles. Mrs. Jane, your Mama, she'd roll her eyes and shake her head every time he had a new one."

"So that's why Papa left this poem. He wanted me to solve the riddle. Was he always doing things like that?"

"If you have a poem from him, there's no question about it. Mr. MacEve's motto was, 'If they're not interested enough to work the solution, they don't deserve the answer.' 'Develops the brain,' he'd say. Come, there's something I want to show you."

"I can't, Mrs. Knotty warned me to stay here."

"Is she the lady with that big hat? The butler told me they were allowed in. I don't know why."

"I do, but I want to know about Mama and Papa."

"We can get you out without her seeing us."

"Listen!" whispered Peggy, "I think she's coming."

"Can you keep a secret?"

"Oh yes. I have many secrets. You'd be surprised what I know."

"Well keep this one for sure. I'm going to hide. You wait," whispered Miss Finney, and she disappeared behind a secret door just as Mrs. Knotty returned.

"So you are alone. I thought I heard voices," questioned Mrs. Knotty with a look of doubt.

"No doubt you did," replied Peggy. "There's probably people hidden behind the walls."

"Don't be so ridiculous! You stay here and mind your manners," scoffed Mrs. Knotty, and left.

Miss Finney came out and motioned for Peggy to follow. "Watch your step, it's dark. I wouldn't want you to fall on the stairs. Hold my hand."

"This is a secret passage!" exclaimed Peggy.

"Yes," said Miss Finney as they came to the kitchen, and from there, they hurried on to the Guest Room. Miss Finney opened a chest and pulled out a small painting. "This is you with your Mama and Papa."

Peggy stood speechless as she held it, trying to remember the occasion. She studied the image of her Mama's long hair, her bright blue eyes, and very stylish dress. Her Papa was thin, but stood tall, looking proud; one hand around her Mama, and the other on Peggy's shoulder. Peggy stood silent with tears rolling down her cheeks.

Miss Finney took a handkerchief from her sleeve.

"I'm sorry. It must be difficult for you, I thought it might help," she consoled.

"Don't feel sorry. I need to see this," assured Peggy. "Look how small I was. I've grown older."

"Of course you have. You're becoming a young lady. Before you know it, you'll be all grown up."

Somehow it was different than what Peggy had expected. She was thrilled to have found her family, but still couldn't remember. It was a strange feeling.

"Are those Mama's clothes?" she asked as she held a beautiful dress to her heart.

"Yes. Your Papa insisted they had far too much and must leave some things behind."

Peggy quickly went through the entire chest. Every item sent shivers down her spine. After putting everything back, Peggy still held onto the picture. Suddenly, Miss Finney exclaimed, "Oh, my dear! We better get back to the chapel, but I just remembered something about you!"

"What is it?" asked Peggy with excitement.

"Nothing significant, just your favourite candy. Do you want some?"

"I guess I do!"

"We have lots. We better hurry," said Miss Finney as she led Peggy back to the kitchen. "Here, take this bag of taffy. It is your favourite."

Peggy took a piece, and began chewing.

"Yummy, it is so good! Thank you, and not just for the taffy, but for all that you've done," said Peggy as she put the bag of taffy into her pocket.

"You're more than welcome. Come, I'll take you back to the chapel."

"How do you know Mrs. Knotty won't see us coming through the secret door?"

"I'll show you how. Let's go."

As they approached the secret door, Miss Finney stopped, and pointed to three little pinholes that gave different views, showing if anyone was in the chapel. "Now you take a look for yourself," she whispered.

Peggy bent down checking the view. "That's amazing," she whispered as she looked through each hole. She checked through the middle hole again, the one that showed the door from the hall to the chapel. To her horror, Mrs. Knotty entered and looked around. They heard her call Hope's name. She waited. With no response, Mrs. Knotty dashed back out the door.

"Mrs. Knotty just left," whispered Peggy to Miss Finney. "Quick. Sneak back to your chair before she returns. I'll go to the kitchen through the passage."

Miss Finney opened the secret door while Peggy quickly slipped to her chair, sitting quietly as if she had never left. Minutes later Mrs. Knotty rushed back, shocked to see Peggy. "Where were you? I thought I told you to stay in this room and not to move," she demanded.

"Remember I told you about people hiding in the walls, I joined them," smiled Peggy.

"Don't be a smart mouth and lie to me, you insolent child. You were hiding behind the door weren't you? I should have looked there."

"Whatever you say, Mrs. Knotty."

"No more saucy words or you'll be more than sorry. I'll be back in a minute, and don't you dare move again," she threatened as she left and hastened down the hall.

Peggy heard her speak in a tense voice.

"It's getting late, Oliver. You'd better find that chest and fast."

"I've been searching like a hawk. It's not my fault I can't find it."

"I bet Frank could find it," she taunted, hoping her comment would provoke Oliver to search harder.

"I've had enough of your nagging. I'm going to the cellar!" grumbled Mr. Knotty, not knowing where else to look, and hoping to find something to quench his thirst.

In the cellar, cobwebs tangled around his face, but the cool air soothed his flaming temper. Rows of bottles stood lined up on a number of shelves. *Ah! At last,* thought Oliver. Unfortunately, every one was empty, causing him to become more irritated. He found a cupboard and quickly opened the door. The rank smell turned his nose. A dead rat lay at the bottom of a large bottle.

"What next!" he muttered in disgust, quickly shutting the door to conceal the putrid odor before he took another breath. Now frantic, he turned in every direction, searching for the slightest clue for something to drink. The lantern lit an object about the size of a chest, tucked in a dark corner, covered with a canvas.

"Finally, a wine cask," he sighed while yanking off the covering. His eyes widened to the size of saucers. His radiant face almost glowed in the dark. There, in bold type, was the name F. MacEve.

Sudden footsteps startled him; he rushed, covering the chest before the unexpected visitor arrived. "Well, now! What do we have here?" inquired Mr. Betts, with revenge in his eyes.

"Mr. Betts, how did you get in here?" asked Oliver, shocked and terrified.

"I told the butler I had an urgent message for you. Isn't it my good fortune that his poor widowed niece lives near my home? I'm sure my promise to have her leaky roof fixed persuaded him to let me in."

"I'm relieved to tell you I have your money. I apologize for being late, but unforeseen circumstances prevented me from fulfilling my commitment. I'm sure you understand," he hastened to add with a trembling voice.

Mr. Betts tipped back his hat and remained silent while shaking his head. Oliver began to quake; the sign of Mr. Betts tipping back his hat meant Oliver had crossed the line. He read the message loud and clear. It was too late for apologies, but he made one last desperate attempt.

"Mr. Betts, please! We've adopted a young girl. She has a large inheritance. Look, I think that's the treasure," he assured and pulled off the canvas. "I wanted to have it in hand before contacting you. You must believe me."

"Mr. Knotty, if word leaked out that I was merciful to anyone with an overdue account, I'd have no control over my business affairs. You knew the conditions."

"Please! Mr. Betts. I won't say a word. Nobody will know," he pleaded, with perspiration pouring from his forehead.

"My men would know. Now let's get it over with."

"No! Please! Take *all* my inheritance, only spare me."

"All?"

"Yes all."

"Hmm! Let me see what you have inside that chest."

"Yes, of course," he replied with a glimmer of hope, "but it's locked and I don't have the key. I was searching for something to smash it open," he insisted as he kneeled, yanking at the lock with his bare hands.

Mr. Betts didn't say a word. He reached inside his suit coat and pulled out a pistol. "Please, I'm begging you Mr. Betts," pleaded Oliver still on his knees. "I thought we had a deal."

Mrs. Knotty, furious over Oliver's delay, went searching for him. She made her way to the cellar and upon arriving, saw the back of Mr. Betts through the doorway. She heard Oliver's plea as Mr. Betts took aim and fired. She charged from behind, knocking Mr. Betts to the floor and stumbling beside him. Before he had a chance to sit up, Mrs. Knotty jammed her foot against his neck, threatening to break it if he so much as moved.

Oliver was still on his knees shaking and biting his fingernails. He jumped up and ran over to grab the gun, hoping Hannah hadn't noticed his fearful state. Looking at her husband, Hannah was shocked and relieved to see him alive. Oliver explained that Mr. Betts shot the lock off the chest and didn't shoot him. He took Hannah's cape and handkerchief to tie Mr. Betts.

While Oliver was busy securing Mr. Betts, Mrs. Knotty had a brilliant idea.

"Mr. Betts, you will forgive Mr. Knotty his debt, correct?"

"Never! And that treasure isn't yours any more. Mr. Knotty just handed it over to me."

Instantly Mrs. Knotty pushed harder. Mr. Betts turned red and began to choke.

"Are you sure you won't forgive him, or do I have to push harder?"

"Yes! Yes! Just get your foot off my neck," he croaked.

"Very good, Mr. Betts. Now gag him, Oliver."

After Mr. Betts was tied and gagged, Oliver rushed to the chest.

"So you finally found the inheritance?" said the pleased Mrs. Knotty.

"Yes. Stand back, Hannah!" he shouted, "I'm ready to open it."

His eyes glistened and his heart pounded. "We're going to be rich at last," he announced with glee.

Mr. Betts was kicking and trying to break free with much rolling and shaking. Mr. Knotty looked over at Mr. Betts.

"Never mind him, open that treasure," ordered Mrs. Knotty. I want to get out of this forsaken hole. Those spiders give me the creeps."

Oliver rubbed his hands together while a big smile wrapped around his face.

"Here goes," he yelled, flinging open the lid. Horror, fear, and disbelief gripped his heart. He stood speechless.

"Well! What is it?" questioned Mrs. Knotty, while Mr. Betts rocked back and forth trying to lift his head high enough to see inside.

Oliver remained silent with balls of sweat covering his forehead and tears dripping from of his eyes.

"Coal! Nothing but coal! I don't understand," he wept while scratching his head.

"I've seen it all now," snarled Hannah.

"There's more to this than meets the eye. Peggy must know something about this. Maybe that's why she had that puzzled look on her face when she read the poem. It must be important, that's why her father gave it to her. If you hadn't been so hasty in cutting her off, we would have heard all the words. Where is she anyway? I thought you were staying with her?" Oliver demanded.

"She's in the chapel. I threatened her and she doesn't

know I'm down here trying to hurry you up. We had better return to the chapel now."

As they left, Mr. Betts went into another contortion with all sorts of motions and sounds, eager to be set free, but to no avail.

After Mrs. Knotty threatened Peggy not to leave the chapel, she became absorbed by studying the poem. She raced through every word again. It read:

To Our Dear Hope

As you venture though life,
Welcome freedom, not strife.
Aim for the highest goals,
As treasures within, unfold.

Reach the top, one step at a time,
A tower of strength you must climb.
Stretch forth; hold with one hand,
Or dead on stone you'll land.

Fix your eye on the glorious prize,
Its value is of unimaginable size.
Lord, may no one steal from her,
Let every dream catch her.

The map to your life, wrapped so neat,
Carefully unfold with every heartbeat.
Travel o'er seas in your quest,
Fortunes are facing due west.
My own bay, make your start,
Anchor your ship; do your part.
Tiny seed grows great oak,
The isle your dreams will evoke.

Treasure doesn't lie visibly on land,
Like gold, dig deep below sand.

Others have tried, but failed,
Secrets inside; you'll prevail.

Scotland, not old, but the new,
Is patiently waiting for you.

Your loving Papa, Frederick MacEve.

Will you find your treasure?
Only time will tell.

The connection between New Scotland or Nova Scotia, and Castle Fraise were becoming clearer. As she read the poem again, she did not notice the fading light.

A maid quietly entered the chapel, lit the lamp, and started to leave when she stopped. Peggy glanced toward the maid, who nodded, and was about to speak. The old gentleman, who Mrs. Knotty had earlier almost knocked over, was standing in the doorway. He abruptly cleared his throat as if to tell her to be on her way. Immediately she left. The old gentleman shuffled off behind her.

Farther down the hall, away from Peggy, James forced himself to keep a low voice, "What were you thinking? You can't let her know we're here."

"It looked like she was trembling. I only wanted to let her know we were keeping an eye on her and we'd be around if she needed us."

"Well don't let that happen again!"

"Alright, I'll be more careful," assured Billy.

"Now let's get out of sight. I'm going up the tower. You see if you can find the Knottys."

Peggy continued to study the poem. The phrase, 'A tower of strength you must climb', lured her to the door and beyond. The steep, spiral stairs became more eerie as she climbed. Her shadow followed like a ghostly intruder. Even her footsteps echoed through the hollow of the tower.

At last she stood near the top step and looked down. The sight of the cold stone floor far below caused a churning sensation in her stomach.

'Keep your eye on the prize'. *Where's the prize?* In the dim light she saw an array of Aboriginal objects, neatly displayed on the opposite wall, over the chasm. A dreamcatcher was in the middle of the objects. At that instant Peggy remembered the line in the poem that haunted her, 'Let every dream catch her.' She now understood it was significant. She must get the dreamcatcher. The idea of going over the dreaded rail to get it terrified her, but there was no other choice. Willpower overtook reason and she soon convinced herself by saying, "I will do it."

She gripped the rail with both hands. A cold chill ran through her veins. Slowly she lifted one foot over the rail, looking down only for a safe footing. Fear seized her heart, but fortitude drove her on. Shaking, she lifted the other foot and secured it. Now with her left hand stretched

across the abyss, the dreamcatcher was at her fingertips. Another inch would be enough to capture the elusive prize. She could hear her heart pounding. *If only Billy could see me now, he'd never call me a coward again,* she reasoned.

She gave her right foot a little boost to give enough height to snatch the dreamcatcher. Her fingers and thumb barely caught it when her foot slipped. She dropped. The violent jerk shot excruciating pain through her shoulder. Inwardly she screamed, but only a moan escaped her lips as she swayed, five stories above the cold stone floor. The fingers of her right hand gripped the rail like forged steel while her left hand clutched the dreamcatcher. She struggled to grab the rail with her left hand without losing the dreamcatcher, while trying to find the steps with her heel. She heard footsteps and thought someone was coming to rescue her.

In their search to find Peggy, the Knottys had combed the area. From where they stood at the bottom of the tower, they looked up, and saw Peggy dangling over the rail.

The sight of Peggy struggling to keep the dreamcatcher while clutching the rail caused Mrs. Knotty to suspect the object was of great importance. The Knottys quietly climbed the steps.

"Give me that thing," snarled Mrs. Knotty as she snatched the dreamcatcher from Peggy's hand.

"No! Somebody help! Help!" Peggy's shout echoed down the empty tower.

Peggy was losing her grip when she felt hands grasp her wrists. The voice of Mr. Knotty yelled, "Let go. I can't lift you while you're holding on."

"Oliver wait!" ordered Mrs. Knotty. "This contraption must be very important if she was willing to risk her life. Peggy, this is the key to the inheritance, isn't it?"

For once, Mrs. Knotty called me Peggy, but Peggy didn't answer, she squeezed her eyes tight and pressed her lips together.

"Tell me what I need to know and we'll pull you up!" shouted Mrs. Knotty.

"Help, I'm going to fall," shouted Peggy.

Unable to ignore Peggy's cries, Oliver began to lift her by the wrists.

Earlier, James had been at the top of the stairway and slipped outside the instant he heard Peggy coming. The door was stuck, but he nudged it with his shoulder, releasing it instantly. Now, with Peggy screaming for help, he frantically reached for the door latch, but fumbled in the dark, pushing it through the hole where it dropped to the floor inside. *Great! Just great!* he fumed, while sticking his finger into the latch hole and pulling. It was useless. Quickly he reached down, grabbed his knife, and forced it between the doorjamb and the door. Little by little he inched it open.

"Come on! Come on! Open!" he mumbled to the door.

Just before it finally popped open, Mr. Knotty was ordering Peggy, "Let go, I tell you! Now!"

"Never! I don't trust you," shouted Peggy who gripped both hands on the rail. Her knuckles were white as snow and her teeth clutched tight.

Mr. Knotty, from behind, placed his hands in front of Peggy's shoulders and reached under her arms to pull. Peggy was sure he wanted to drop her and she wasn't taking any chances. She sunk her teeth into his right hand with all her might. "Ouch! You brat!" he yelled, letting go to suck on the bite. A second later, he grabbed Peggy by the wrists where she couldn't bite him.

That's when Mrs. Knotty, who by now was fit to be tied, quickly spoke in an icy voice that Peggy would never forget. "Oliver, let her go!"

Mr. Knotty stood in silent disbelief.

"Drop her now!" ordered Mrs. Knotty.

Mr. Knotty stood aghast, battling between obeying Hannah and his conscience; he was searching for a reason to save Peggy.

"If she's dead, how will we know why that contraption you're holding is important?"

Before Hannah could reply, James leaped through the door, landing beside Mr. Knotty. Mrs. Knotty's mouth flew wide open. That old decrepit man she almost knocked over earlier leaped like a lion. Before she knew it, James raised his dagger and pressed the point against Mr. Knotty's neck. "Drop Peggy and you are a dead man."

Peggy's heart skipped a beat as she heard the sweet voice of James. There was dead silence. Another voice resounded up the tower.

"Hold on Peggy, I'm coming," yelled Billy, pulling the dress up past his knees. He leaped up the steps like a tiger was nipping at his heels. Sweat poured off his brow. Reaching Peggy, he leaned over the rail, gripping her by the waist.

"It's alright. I have you. Let go."

Peggy couldn't see what was going on behind her while she was dangling back on to the stairs. She hesitated to release her grip. "I have you," assured Billy.

"Are you sure?"

"Yes, now let go."

"Here goes," and the instant she let go, her piercing scream made Billy's ears ring. She was heavier than he thought, and the two of them almost tumbled down the abyss. Adrenaline shot through Billy's veins and he heaved Peggy over the rail.

Safely on the step, Peggy instantly turned to Mrs. Knotty, "Give me the dreamcatcher please," she insisted while Mrs. Knotty grudgingly handed it to her.

"Thank you," she said with relief, and looked at Billy. She let out another screech.

"Billy! You? The maid?" she gasped and laughed. Next she saw the old man.

"Yikes! James?" she questioned with eyes bulging.

"It's me alright," assured James who was still holding the dagger against Mr. Knotty's neck.

"Oh, thank you both. I thought I was going to die," she exclaimed as she glanced back and forth to James and Billy.

The sparkle in Billy's eyes, and the curl on his lips, told Peggy he was ecstatic at having rescued her.

While James and Billy were focused on Peggy, Mr. Knotty pulled the pistol he retrieved from Mr. Betts and aimed it at Peggy.

"Take that knife away," he ordered James.

Annoyed with himself for not being more cautious, James slowly, but reluctantly, removed the knife from Mr. Knotty's neck.

"Now Peggy, give Mrs. Knotty the dreamcatcher."

Peggy's anger boiled. The thought of giving Mrs. Knotty her dreamcatcher was more than she could bear. She didn't move.

"I said give it to Mrs. Knotty. Now!"

Peggy wouldn't surrender. With a defiant expression, she clung tightly to the dreamcatcher. Mrs. Knotty was infuriated. She tried to grab the dreamcatcher, but Peggy would not let go. Peggy attempted to run up the stairs while Mrs. Knotty pulled her back, and Peggy lost her balance. In their struggle, Peggy lost her grip on the dreamcatcher, and it fluttered over the edge.

Everyone stood still for two seconds. Peggy's eyebrows raised, her mouth opened and she took a deep breath as she watched in horror, her dreamcatcher floating to the bottom of the tower.

"Why you miserable child," scorned Mrs. Knotty as she grabbed Peggy, who attempted to dash down the steps to retrieve the dreamcatcher. In their bout, they fell against Mr. Knotty, who was forced to grab the rail or roll down the stairs. He accidently pulled the trigger of the pistol.

Click!

Billy, James, and Peggy stood still. Shocked that Mr. Knotty had been bluffing all along, Peggy and Mrs. Knotty made a dash down the steps.

"Don't waste your time Mrs. Knotty," shouted a voice from below.

All eyes looked down. The figure stooped, picked up the dreamcatcher, and stared grinning up at them. It was Mr. Betts.

Peggy clenched her fists and shook her hands in disgust. "Excuse me sir, that dreamcatcher belongs to me. Give it back."

"The only time I saw a fight like that was when a lot of money was at stake. This thing must be worth a fortune. It wouldn't have anything to do with that inheritance, would it?" asked Mr. Betts.

"Give that to me!" ordered Mrs. Knotty. "It's not yours!"

"Mrs. Knotty, I'm afraid you don't understand. Possession is nine-tenths of the law."

"Mr. Betts! I'll help you with that dreamcatcher," shouted Mr. Knotty.

"Ha! You help me? Why would I need your help?"

"Because you are looking death in the eye," threatened Oliver as he aimed the pistol at Mr. Betts.

"I'm coming down, Mr. Betts. Don't move or I'll shoot," he warned with a quivering voice. He began his descent, but his shaking hand revealed his fear.

"Don't be foolish Mr. Knotty. My men will find you and you don't want to even think about what they will do to you and Mrs. Knotty," he replied.

Mr. Betts smiled and opened his suit coat, showing his vest pocket. He patted it. The flask of powder and three lead balls were still there.

"Mr. Knotty, you can't shoot me, the pistol isn't loaded. Remember, you didn't reload it after I blew off that lock. You failed again Mr. Knotty."

Suddenly Mr. Betts listened intently. He heard pounding footsteps running toward him and the voices indicated there was more than one person. Not sure who or what he might encounter, Mr. Betts turned and fled.

At that moment, the butler and Miss Finney raced

through the entrance. They arrived just in time to see Mr. Betts' heels as he ran out the opposite exit.

"Stop him!" shouted Peggy, "He has my dreamcatcher. I must have it."

Mr. Betts challenged them.

"If you want this thing, come get it."

James, Billy, and Peggy raced down the stairs. In the dark, it was impossible to see where Mr. Betts had disappeared.

The butler and Miss Finney looked in all directions, trying to figure out what all the screaming and shouting were about.

"We need a carriage," shouted Peggy.

"Come along. I'll have the stable boys take care of it right away," said the butler.

At that instant, the Knottys made a desperate attempt to vanish.

"Stop them!" yelled Peggy as she turned to the sound of running feet.

Billy and James latched onto them.

"Just where do you think you're going?" James demanded.

Neither answered. That was the first time Peggy had seen Mrs. Knotty speechless.

"James, make them take us to Mr. Betts'. They know where he lives. We must get the dreamcatcher!" insisted Peggy.

"What's so important about the dreamcatcher?" Billy wanted to know.

"I'll tell you later in private. I'm the only one who knows," assured Peggy.

"Well, I'm sure Mr. Knotty would love to show us where Mr. Betts lives," said Billy as he boldly puffed out his chest, pressing his knife against Mrs. Knotty's neck.

"Tell your husband to take us there right away, or would you rather have me accidently slip with this knife?"

"Yes! We'll take you," hastened Mr. Knotty. "I'll show you exactly where he lives. Wouldn't you agree Hannah?"

Mrs. Knotty's head shivered, and her eyes rolled, letting Oliver know he would face the consequences later for his ridiculous question. He tried backtracking by warning Billy, "Now you be careful with that knife young man. One scratch on Mrs. Knotty and the only thing I'll be showing you is trouble."

"Mr. Knotty," said Billy, "do your job, and you won't have to worry about Mrs. Knotty's dainty neck."

Chapter 9
The Chase

With the Knottys forced to show them where Mr. Betts lived, Peggy was impatient to get moving.

"Come on! Hurry up, you two," she urged.

"Not until I get out of this outfit," protested Billy.

"We don't have time," argued Peggy.

"She's right Billy, as much as I'd like to change, it'll have to wait.

"No sir! I'm changing."

"Then you'll be staying here by yourself," assured Peggy, starting on her way with James and Mr. Knotty following.

"What about me?" protested Mrs. Knotty, not moving because Billy's knife was still resting on her neck.

"Billy will just have to take care of you himself," replied Peggy casually, knowing Billy wouldn't be long changing his mind about coming with them.

"Not on your life," he protested, while marching behind, and pushing Mrs. Knotty, to catch up.

"I hope nobody recognizes me," he grumbled.

"Who do you know in Scotland that would recognize you?" asked Peggy, keeping ahead so Billy couldn't see her laughing. She was sure James was doing the same.

At the stable, Mrs. Knotty's irritation increased to a higher level when Billy's knife touched her pretty neck.

"Take that thing away from me!" she insisted.

"I will when you are tied and can't escape. Peggy, tie their hands."

"With pleasure."

Mrs. Knotty kept blaming Oliver for his stupidity and complained about being humiliated by these disrespectful brats.

After binding the Knottys, James and Billy wasted no time helping the stable boys prepare Chestnut and the carriage for the chase.

"That's it, we're ready. Let's go," said Billy.

"Mr. Knotty, you sit up here with me. Peggy, you and Billy stay inside the carriage with Mrs. Knotty," instructed James, "But first help me with Mr. Knotty, Billy. He can't climb up with his hands tied behind his back."

"Now it's your turn Mrs. Knotty," said Peggy, "We'll help you to climb inside."

"Get your grubby hands off me! I'll take care of myself," she snapped, and almost fell on her face before finally making it inside the carriage.

"We're ready James, let's go," said Billy.

A blanket of dense fog drifting from the River Don covered the winding road to Aberdeen. Travel was slow and hazardous. Finally, on the outskirts of town, Mr. Knotty, now shaking, and with perspiration running down his face, quietly gave directions.

"Stop here!" he whispered. "See that road with a row of trees on both sides? It leads directly to Mr. Betts' farmhouse. It's the one you can barely see, set well back from the road."

"We don't need these two any more," said Billy quietly as he stuck his head out the window to speak to James. "Let's dump them."

"We might need them later. Let's put Mr. Knotty inside the carriage too. There's rope under my seat. Tie their feet too and gag them," said James.

Just up the street from Mr. Betts' home, the three

adventurers found a field with a huge overhanging tree. It was the perfect spot to hide Chestnut and the carriage.

"Now let's go to Mr. Betts' place," encouraged Billy. "I'm anxious to get that dreamcatcher and be on our way home."

"You're not the only one Billy," agreed James.

Approaching Mr. Betts' house, Billy was full of suggestions.

"Let's split up, see what we can find out, and meet back here in a few minutes. Then we'll decide how to catch Mr. Betts off guard to get the dreamcatcher back. James, you and Peggy take the back, I'll check through the front windows."

Billy snooped around, checking this window and that. He spotted two goons inside; Mr. Betts was nowhere to be seen. Just when he started congratulating himself for his fine detective work, a rough hand forcefully covered his mouth, and another hand rested on his shoulder.

"Hello miss. Are you looking for me?" whispered a soft voice in Billy's ear. He cringed when he felt a rough cheek rub against his.

"No sir, Mr. Betts," he squeaked in his best attempt to imitate a female voice.

"What the..." jumped the goon. "Look at me!" he shouted. "What are you, man or woman?"

Billy turned, covering his face with one hand.

"Answer me!" threatened the goon, and pulled something from his belt. A cold barrel embedded itself against Billy's temple.

"Man sir!" he quickly replied.

"Man! What're ya doin' dressin' like a woman? If this is some kind'a joke, you picked the wrong guy to play it on," he growled while squeezing Billy's arm.

"It's a long story, sir. But first, please take that gun away."

"I'll decide when to take it away, you weasel. Do as I say and maybe I won't blow a hole in that puny brain of yours."

Billy didn't reply, but nodded in agreement as he

warily headed around the house where this goon was steering him. It was the same path that Peggy and James had taken just moments earlier. Suddenly, Billy cringed at the sound of furious dogs barking and snarling in the back yard where he was being forced to go. All he pictured was being the next victim. In a minute he expected to be half, if not totally dead, like the mauled bodies of Peggy and James.

While Billy had been out front, Peggy and James had crept toward the rear door when they heard the ferocious dogs rushing toward them. The silence of the night was shattered by the most violent hullabaloo one could imagine.

"Uh-oh!" whispered Peggy.

"They're coming fast. Quick! Up here!" replied James.

He grabbed Peggy and threw her onto the porch rooftop. Two large, vicious dogs charged around the corner, barking, snarling, and growling. Their lips curled, showing huge fangs that glistened in the dark, with saliva dripping from their mouths.

Horrified that James was about to be mauled to death, Peggy's instinct was to jump to his rescue, but without a weapon to beat off the dogs, she reasoned it was senseless for both of them to be mangled. Helplessly, she watched.

James leaped onto a pile of stacked barrels beside the house, only to feel them give way. With his arms flailing and his feet hopping from one rolling barrel to the next, he barely evaded the dogs, with their jaws snapping at his feet.

The dogs leaped and yelped, but were unable to tear into him. James' skillful act ended when the barrel he was rolling on struck something; coming to a sudden halt and driving him head first into a nearby haystack. The dogs rushed forward ready to gorge. James groped around, searching for protection. With nothing else close at hand he grabbed the barrel, darted forward, backward, and from side to side to thwart off the seething dogs. The fact that they were unable to feast on James' legs only agitated the dogs all the more.

Two men rushed from the house and stood watching, amused. James was about to collapse when the men decided they had enough entertainment and called off the vicious creatures.

"Well lookee here, Cage."

"Yeah, I'm looking. What've we got, Tripp?"

"I'm not sure. I never saw any old man jump and hop like that. I wonder what he does to stay so nimble?" asked Tripp.

"Let's find out."

"Tell us old man, how do you stay so active? We'd like to know." asked Tripp.

"Well, it's like this," began James, but that was all that Tripp needed to hear. He pinched James' lips together, preventing him from continuing, and held a lantern close to his face for a better look.

"I think we've got ourselves another scoundrel," breathed Tripp into James' face. The stench from the man's breath was so foul, James had to turn his head away before gagging. Tripp continued, "This is no old man. He's just a young ram."

"Really!" doubted Cage, whose dim eyesight caused him to examine James within inches of his face.

"Well, I'll be a monkey's uncle! You're right, Tripp. So much for us, learnin' how to stay young. Who're you and what're you doin' snoopin' around in Mr. Betts' back yard?" he demanded suspiciously.

"I'm James sir," he coughed, gasping for fresh air. "I'm looking for Mr. Betts." I have business to discuss with him. Is he home?"

"Business, aye! I bet you do. What kind of business?"

Before James had a chance to answer, Grub was pushing Billy around from the opposite corner of the house where he had heard the dogs begin their rampage. He had expected to witness the fierce battle he'd soon join, when abrupt silence indicated that Peggy and James had met their doom. Seeing James in one piece and without a scratch put a big smile on Billy's face. James was totally confused and couldn't understand why Billy was so happy.

"Here's another one. I wonder where that girl is?" questioned Grub.

"What's wrong with you, Grub? Gone blind? You got the girl," howled Cage.

"Yeah! Fooled me too. That's no girl. Says his name is Billy. He's looking for Mr. Betts. I bet he'll be sorry he found him," mocked Grub.

"This feller says he's looking for the boss too. They must be two of the three the boss told us to watch out for. I think we'll be in for a bonus after catching these two," said Cage with glee.

"Not without the girl, you won't. She's the one the boss really wants," reminded Tripp.

Peggy, still crouched on the porch roof, recognized Grub's voice. He was the creepy man who had grabbed Mr. Knotty by the coattail and warned him to pay up. It was obvious he was in charge.

"We'll tie them and leave them in the stable. Tripp, you stay to keep an eye on these two. We wouldn't want'em to miss their appointment with Mr. Betts," laughed Grub.

After tying James and Billy, Cage and Grub sauntered toward the house.

"Mr. Betts will be asking about a little girl," said Grub, "We better take a look around."

"She's gotta be around here somewhere," agreed Cage as they passed directly below Peggy.

Peggy kept well hidden as they passed beneath her. She wondered if Grub was his real name. Whatever the case, the poor fellow looked like a bulldog. She felt sorry for him. After all, nobody would want a face like that unless they were dressed for a masquerade.

"I'll go tell the boss we have those two tied up in the barn," said Grub. "You keep your eye out for that girl."

At the end of the house, on the second floor, Grub approached Mr. Betts' office. He announced, "We have good news boss."

"I'm glad to hear that. Do you have the girl?" he asked with optimism.

"No, but we got them other two varmints tied up in the barn. They said they had important business with you."

"What about the girl?"

"Not a sign of her."

"Find her! She'll be more than happy to tell me why this contraption is important when I get my hands on her," he growled as he held up the dreamcatcher. "I can't get my money without her. Do I make myself clear?"

"Yes sir! We'll find her."

"It's late and I'm tired. I'm going to bed. I don't want to be disturbed unless you get the girl. I expect we'll have a busy day tomorrow. I don't want any slip-ups either. Do you understand?"

"Yes Mr. Betts. You can count on us," assured Grub.

Cage and Grub combed the area for over an hour without finding Peggy. They passed beneath her several times, but never thought of looking up. She was well hidden in the shadows. It was getting late, cold, and damp. On top of that, she was hungry.

Then she remembered the taffy that Miss Finney had given her; it was still in her pocket. She took a piece, hoping it would ease her hunger pains while waiting for everyone to go to sleep. She savoured the flavor and began chewing. It stuck to her teeth, which gave her a brilliant idea.

It was only a few hours before daylight when Peggy was finally convinced Mr. Betts and his men were sound asleep. She shimmied down the porch post to the ground.

Under the porch, next to the house, was a stack of wood. She grabbed a block and stepped toward the barn. The dogs stood and perked up their ears. Peggy wanted to knock them out cold, but knew she couldn't hit both of them at the same time. She questioned if her idea would work.

She took little pieces of taffy that she had broken off while on the roof and tossed them to the dogs as she approached. They looked suspiciously at her, then down at the treat. One dog sniffed it, which was enough to make the other follow suit. To Peggy's surprise and delight, they snatched it into their mouths, and began chewing as if they were in doggy heaven. She threw pieces a few feet closer to herself each time, coaxing them from the door to where she stood. They were now within reach.

"You enjoy this big piece. I'll give you more when we leave," she whispered.

Those two ferocious dogs were now smacking and curling their lips in all sorts of contortions. Their tongues rolled and slurped from one side to another, up, down, and around. Their heads shook; but the delicious taffy remained stuck to their teeth.

It was time to make her move. Peggy stole inside the stable door. There was Tripp, fast asleep in a chair, with his head nestled against a pile of hay. He looked so peaceful. *I hope he doesn't wake,* Peggy thought, as she took another step that landed her right beside him.

One of the dogs must have bitten his tongue because he let out a sharp yelp and little whimper. Tripp jerked, muttered, and rubbed his eyes. Peggy stood beside him with the block of wood held above his head, just in case. After a good face rubbing, his eyeballs opened to the size of saucers. "What...?" was all he managed to utter before Peggy knocked him into a deeper sleep than the one from which he had just woken.

"I'm sorry I had to do that, Tripp. I hope it didn't hurt too much," she said as she leaned over and patted the sore spot. "That should make it all better."

"Never mind patting his head, get over here and untie us," whispered Billy.

"Don't order me around, Billy! Do you know how

many times I've wanted to do that to you? You'd better behave or I'll practice on you," she gleamed.

"Alright! Alright! Remember, I saved your neck, too. Just cut us free."

"Yes, you did, didn't you; I am thankful for that."

"Take the knife from inside my pant leg," said James.

"Boy! Are we lucky they didn't see you," sighed Billy.

"We aren't out of here yet," warned James. "I hope those dogs like you better than me."

"I took care of them. Right now they are finishing a nice meal of taffy. I have more to feed them on our way out. Maybe they'd like a chunk of you instead, eh Billy?" teased Peggy.

"Nope, I'm sure you're wrong *this time,* but I have no intention of finding out."

As they crept through the stable door, the two contented dogs were still licking their chops, but the candy was devoured. "They still look hungry to me. Throw them some more," urged Billy.

Both dogs ran toward Peggy for another course. Billy caught a glimpse of their shiny ivories as they opened wide to snatch their prize. He grasped Peggy's hand to drag her away. The dogs growled with curled lips, warning him not to harm their friend. A chill ran down Billy's back.

"Nice doggies, nice doggies, eat your taffy," coaxed Billy as he slowly let go of Peggy's hand and crept away.

Peggy then gave each dog another piece of taffy. She saved a couple of pieces, just in case. Carefully she made her way, catching up to James and Billy. Relieved and at a safe distance, Peggy asked, "How are we going to get my dreamcatcher? Mr. Betts has it. From what I know, his office is at the end of the house. The guy named Grub headed that way to tell Mr. Betts they caught you two."

"There's no way we can get up to Betts' office without getting caught," insisted Billy.

"There must be a way," argued Peggy. "Mr. Betts wouldn't sleep in his office. Let's at least look. I'm going, are you coming with me?" asked Peggy as she started toward the end of the house.

"I think she lost her mind from lack of sleep, James. Stop her!"

"You know what happened when we tried to take her from the Knottys. You lost your pants. I'm going to have a look, too."

"You're both losing it from lack of sleep," resolved Billy as he followed behind.

At the end of Mr. Betts' house was a door. It was locked. "How are we going to get in?" whispered Billy.

Without saying a word, Peggy pointed to the open window on the second floor; it was Mr. Betts' office.

Billy shook his head.

"No! No! I can't climb the wall."

Peggy motioned like she was climbing a ladder and pointed to the stable.

Billy pointed his finger to his head and nodded, indicating Peggy had another good idea. "If I wasn't so tired, I would have thought of that before you," he said quietly.

Peggy rolled her eyes and said, "Sure Billy," and continued on her way, pulling out the last two pieces of taffy before reaching the stable.

"Here goes," she whispered and gave the dogs the taffy.

Billy and James crept quickly inside the stable. In no time, they were back with the ladder. The dogs were enjoying the last of their taffy while the three slinked off. Half way to Mr. Betts' office, Billy glanced over his shoulder. By the light of the lantern, he was relieved to see the dogs stroll over and lay beside Tripp, who was still out cold.

Reaching Mr. Betts' office, James and Billy gently placed the ladder directly below the second story window. Peggy stepped to the ladder to begin her climb when Billy put his arm out to stop her.

"Let me go," he whispered.

Peggy shook her head in disagreement.

"Sorry, but you're too clumsy," she said, and silently climbed the ladder, slipped through the window, and was safely inside. It was too dark to see anything. She waited, hoping her eyes would adjust, but still she couldn't see her dreamcatcher. As a last resort, she lit a match. Across the room, on the end of Mr. Betts' desk was her dreamcatcher. She stepped as quickly as possible without extinguishing the match. Gently picking up the dreamcatcher she started toward the window when suddenly she heard movement from the next room. *I hope the flickering light from the match didn't wake Mr. Betts,* she thought, when the voice of Mr. Betts rang out.

"Who's there?"

Peggy blew out the match, and treaded softly toward the window. She tripped on a mat.

"Grub and Cage! We got company. Get the dogs, and check outside my office! Don't let them escape!" yelled Mr. Betts. He started toward his office with a lamp. Shadows moved along the wall. Peggy scurried toward the open window, but before she could reach it, Mr. Betts entered the room. So near was he to the window, he could have caught her before she could climb out. All she could do was throw out the dreamcatcher.

"Catch the dreamcatcher," she yelled to James and Billy as she threw it. Mr. Betts dove to grab Peggy, but she ducked and darted from under him.

James caught the dreamcatcher.

"I'm going in after her," said Billy as he charged up the ladder. On first glance through the window, Billy spied Mr. Betts holding a lamp and chasing Peggy out from behind his large desk. It was too wide for him to reach across and catch her.

"You won't get away so you might as well give up now. I'll make it easier for you if you co-operate," he promised.

"No way!" shouted Peggy as she made a dash from behind the desk, and ran toward the hall that led to the steps.

Mr. Betts made another lunge for Peggy.

"Stop!" yelled Billy as he stuck his head through the open window.

Mr. Betts turned; shocked to see that girl who had a man's voice. He shook his fist at Billy who now had his shoulders inside as well. The distraction gave Peggy enough time to reach the hall and race down the steps.

"Why you miserable whatever you are," shouted Mr. Betts as he realized his mistake.

"Why don't you try to catch me," taunted Billy. Mr. Betts looked at Billy and then back to Peggy who was disappearing. He raced after her.

Billy hopped down the ladder, two rungs at a time. He kept stepping on his silly dress, almost tripping backwards. "Peggy is running downstairs James. Meet her at the front door!" he yelled while still struggling with his dress.

James tore off.

"Finally!" muttered Billy as his feet hit the ground. He darted to catch up to James, but the dress caught on a peg that was drilled into one side of the ladder. It was used for holding a bucket, but in the dark Billy and James paid no attention and by mistake had placed the ladder upside down. The ladder jerked and came tumbling down, hitting Billy against his leg.

"Let go you miserable thing," he ordered, while grabbing the dress and with one quick jerk, ripped it free.

Peggy raced down the steps, through the parlor, and ran to the front door. She yanked on the handle. The door was bolted shut. Frantically she wiggled the bolt, trying to unlock it before Mr. Betts caught her. She heard James on the outside yelling for her to open the door. She was ready to swing it open when Mr. Betts yelled, "Stop!" She glanced over her shoulder as the knife whizzed past. Terrified, she jumped aside from the threat. The knife was buried deep into the door. Quickly, Peggy wiggled and pulled the knife, flashing it before Mr. Betts' eyes as he approached.

"Get back," she warned.

"Give me that knife," yelled Mr. Betts.

James, hearing Mr. Betts' demand, kicked the door wide open. Peggy dashed out, and the two of them fled.

"Wait for me!" yelled Billy as he tore off around the house with one hand holding his dress high above his knees while his pantaloons fluttered in the breeze. He struggled to catch up, and after reaching them, latched onto Peggy with his free hand. He and James half carried, and half dragged her as they ran for their lives. Billy stumbled as he fought with his dress, which kept getting tangled in his feet.

They feared the dogs, which were now on their trail. Grub was yelling, "Sick'em Rip! Get'em Tear!"

"Rip and Tear!" panted Billy. "I don't like the thought of that. Faster, Peggy, faster!"

The barking and snarling was getting closer, followed by Grub and Cage, with Mr. Betts straggling behind, still in his nightgown.

"Don't let them get away," he yelled as exhaustion forced him to stop, gasping for breath.

"There's the carriage!" shouted James as they made their way to it. He leaped onto the seat, Billy untied the horse like a madman while Peggy opened the door and charged through it, slamming it shut. She stuck her head out the window and yelled, "The Knottys are gone!"

"We can't do anything about that now. Hold on, we're gonna fly outta here!" shouted James.

Billy released Chestnut and had one foot and one hand on the carriage when James cracked the whip. It sounded like a gunshot. He yelled, "Go, Chestnut, go!"

Chestnut leaped forward driving Peggy against the back of the seat inside the carriage. Billy tried pulling his leg away from the jaws of Rip. Rip made a leap for his left foot.

"EEOUCH, James! Move it! He's got me!" yelled Billy.

"Hurry, James! Tear is coming at me too."

"Yaw, yaw, Chestnut!" bellowed James. Chestnut's unexpected burst of speed left Tear biting the dust.

"I gotta shake this beast off!" hollered Billy as he violently shook his leg and struggled to hold on. "That thing is too heavy. He's dragging me off!"

Peggy leaned out the door.

"James, give me the whip!" she shouted.

James let the thin end dangle where Peggy could reach it. Instantly she pulled it inside and leaned out the door again, holding on with only one hand. The bouncing carriage made it almost impossible, but eventually she wedged the whip handle against Rip's frothing teeth. "Let go!" she screamed. Rip snarled, and growled, but hung on while still glaring at Peggy.

"Knock him off, Peggy, I'm losing my grip!" yelled Billy.

James, in an effort to keep Billy from falling, grabbed for his shoulder, but missed and caught him by the bosom.

"Hey! Watch it!" yelled Billy.

"Sorry ma'am. I was aiming for your shoulder!" laughed James, although the situation was still tense.

Peggy leaned out the door even farther, to give a

harder push against Rip's teeth. When she did, he let out a yelp, and snapped at the whip. The instant his mouth opened, he slowed down, and spun around. The rear wheel caught the tip of his tail, causing him to let out one awful howl.

Rip's sudden release left Peggy with no support and she lost her balance. Her hand swung around and smashed against the side of the carriage. She didn't dare let go of the whip. Unfortunately as her hand swung around, so did the whip, which smacked Billy on the back of his head.

"Ouch! Not me! The dog!" he shouted.

"I'm sorry Billy. I couldn't help it," apologized Peggy.

"Yeah right," he laughed while he grabbed James' hand and they pulled together, yanking Billy safely to the seat. He was so relieved to be free from Rip's jaws, he shouted, "Ye haw! Fine job you two!"

"I guess I'm not so bad after all, eh Billy?" said Peggy as she continued talking to them with her head stuck through the window.

"Well in this case, but just remember, if it wasn't for your shenanigans, we wouldn't be in this mess."

"But you wouldn't be having as much fun either!"

"Fun! You call almost being eaten by dogs fun?"

"Alright you too. Settle down," smiled James. "You have to admit Billy that was rather exciting."

"That's because it wasn't your foot. But yeah, you should have seen the look on Betts' face when I yelled at him through the window. He heard a man's voice and saw me with this silly bonnet on. No wonder he was shocked."

"See? Now aren't you glad you didn't have time to change?" roared Peggy.

"Only for the look on Betts' face," sighed Billy as he nursed his sore foot. "It's a good thing Rip didn't latch on above my boot. That beast had one powerful set of jaws! Say, when are we going to find out what's so important about that dreamcatcher? We should be far enough away by now."

"You're right," agreed James, who slowed Chestnut to a trot and rode on a little farther.

"James, stop so I can open the dreamcatcher," insisted Peggy.

"Open it?" questioned Billy, "What's there to open?"

"You'll see," gleamed Peggy, remembering the words, *'The map to your life, wrapped so neat. Carefully unfold with every heartbeat.'*

"Well hurry up, I'm dying to see what's so important about the thing," urged Billy.

"Hold the lamp close," instructed Peggy.

Curious eyes watched as she studied the threads tightly wrapped around the top half of the dreamcatcher. "I need a sharp knife."

Simultaneously two knives flashed beside Peggy's hand. She looked at them both, glancing first at Billy, then to James. She reached for her choice.

"Thank you, Billy," she said and couldn't help but give a little smile.

Billy was happy that Peggy chose his knife. She had forgiven him for hurting Hector. James was shocked, but pleased that Peggy and Billy were getting along so well. He figured his Ma's good principles had sunk in.

Carefully snipping the knots, she began unraveling the thread. A neatly wrapped strip of paper clung to the wood, having been confined there for a number of years. Gently peeling back one corner, she removed the stained message. Her trembling fingers forced the curled paper to lie flat on her knee. Every eye focused on the message that read, 'Congratulations. Here's another clue. Three steps below rock, a secret passage will unlock.'

"Great! Another ridiculous riddle! What kind of dumb joke is this, anyway?" scoffed Billy, who made no secret about his frustration. "Now what are we supposed to do? I knew this inheritance was too good to be true. We're just a bunch of losers chasing a pot of gold at the end of a rainbow. You might as well face it, Peggy; you're never going to be rich."

"You're absolutely wrong, Billy. I know exactly what this clue means. We must go back to Castle Fraise."

"It's too late tonight, it'll be morning before we get there. And who knows how long it'll take to find whatever you're looking for. Another stupid clue, probably," fumed Billy.

"Come on, let's go," encouraged Peggy. "What's the point of leaving without finding the answer to the clue?"

Billy, who still wasn't functioning as well as James and Peggy without his sleep, found his nerves were on edge.

"If I don't get some sleep, you won't have to worry about Mr. Betts and the Knottys," warned Billy emphatically. "Compared to me, they'll look like angels."

"You know, Billy, you don't have to go with us. You could go back to the *Senora*, and catch up on your rest," suggested Peggy.

"Why don't we all get some sleep, and go to the castle in the morning. Come on James, tell me that isn't the best idea yet."

"Billy has a good point."

"If you're that tired, why not sleep on the way," suggested Peggy.

"And just who do you expect to drive?" argued Billy.

"We could take turns," reasoned Peggy.

"I'll go, but I'm not driving," assured Billy.

"I'll drive! Both of you boys can sleep."

"Boys? You drive?" shrieked Billy. "I couldn't sleep a wink with you driving! Hah! You're out of your mind!"

"Well, I'm not coming all this way without meeting Colonel and Mrs. MacEve. And another thing, this dreamcatcher was made by Sarah's Grandpa. See, here are his initials: O.K."

"No kidding. Let me see," said James. Billy crowded closer to have a look.

"Well, I still think it's a waste of time," said Billy.

"I'm staying until I find the answers, and spend time with the MacEves. If you don't like that, you'll have to go without me."

"Well, I guess that settles that. If it's that important, I'll go with you," sighed James. "How about it Billy, you coming?"

"Well, I like the castle, and I'd love to see the look on Peggy's face when she finds another joke."

While the three were fleeing from Mr. Betts and his goons, there was another surprise for Mr. Betts. After Tear missed his attempt to grip Billy's leg, he shook the dust off his fur. He sniffed the air and the ground, and then let out a low steady growl. The fur on his back stood on end as he crouched toward a pile of bushes. Grub arrived just in time to see Tear sniff his way behind the bushes and go into a fury. Mr. Knotty was yelling his head off while Mrs. Knotty pounded at the beast with her handbag. Tear had Mr. Knotty by the pant leg. The two of them were spinning and hopping.

"Call him off," shouted Mr. Knotty, when in one of his spins he caught a glimpse of Grub.

"Don't move, when I call off Tear, or you won't move again," warned Grub as he pointed his pistol.

"We won't budge," promised Mr. Knotty.

Grub called off Tear, and by now Cage was beside them. They waited for Mr. Betts.

"Well! Well! We meet again Mr. Knotty. It seems you are destined to be in my clutches. Take them to the barn. We can do our business there," instructed Mr. Betts as they all silently marched inside the barn. Tripp was rubbing his head; still dazed from the blow Peggy had given him.

Poor Mr. Knotty was shaking and sweating. Mrs. Knotty stood tall, and looked straight into Mr. Betts' eyes.

"Mr. Betts, before you go any further, perhaps we can work something out."

"Work something out! It's a little late for that, Mrs. Knotty!"

"Mr. Betts, your business is with me. Let my wife go," insisted Mr. Knotty.

"Oliver, say nothing. I know what I'm doing," interrupted Hannah. Now Mr. Betts, I'm sure you would like to see your business expand. Why don't you at least listen to my idea?"

"We have lots of time. What did you have in mind?" asked Mr. Betts, who was quite taken with this stunning, bold woman. He was willing to listen, more out of curiosity than agreement.

"We should co-operate to find this Hope MacEve, or Peggy character, so we both benefit, don't you agree?"

"Co-operate! You have a short memory. I wouldn't call threatening to choke me to death with your foot, co-operation."

"I understand perfectly," agreed Mrs. Knotty. "But if we are to succeed, we will have to put the past behind us."

"And what benefit would it be to me, if per chance we are unsuccessful in capturing Miss MacEve, or worse still, the money? The way I see it, Mr. Knotty is free of his debt and I am the loser. You see my predicament!"

"Absolutely! But there is a way to repay Oliver's debt if all else fails."

"I'm listening Mrs. Knotty, go on."

"With your importing and exporting business, you must have a tremendous amount of legal work. Oliver could pay off his debt by performing all your legal matters."

"Do you have any idea how long that would take?" frowned Mr. Betts.

"I'm sure your legal expenses are considerable, Mr. Betts. Besides, there is the good chance of capturing Hope MacEve and you know what that will be worth!"

"You have a point there alright," agreed Mr. Betts.

"Thank you Mr. Betts, but I'm not finished. Do you realize the benefits of having a shrewd lady working in partnership with you?"

"I can't say I do. I've never even considered the matter."

"Well let me assure you. You will not be disappointed."

"You seem pretty sure of yourself."

"You will be too, just try it for six months. That's all I'm asking."

"How do I know you two won't just up and flee, like Mr. Knotty did when he went after Peggy?"

"If he fled, he wouldn't be back here now, would he?"

"You are a clever lady," said Mr. Betts. "What about you Mr. Knotty? Do you agree with this arrangement?"

All eyes focused on Mr. Knotty who was still nervous, but began to calm after listening to Hannah, and seeing Mr. Betts even considering the arrangement.

"Well, Oliver," said Mrs. Knotty with a stare that meant he better say yes, if he expected to see the light of day.

"By all means," he agreed, but underneath dreaded the thought of being under the scrutiny of Mr. Betts.

"Welcome aboard Mrs. Knotty, and you too Oliver," said Mr. Betts as they shook hands.

Chapter 10
Return to Castle Fraise

James took the first shift at driving as they headed for Castle Fraise.

"Billy, you can sleep now," smiled James.

"Thanks old boy! Be sure to wake me up before your eyes fall shut," said Billy, not wanting to look like a weakling.

"For sure," agreed James.

Peggy and Billy slept like babies. James didn't have the heart to wake them, so drove on, even when his head dropped. He kept resting one eye, and then the other. Then both. The next thing he knew, the carriage came to a sudden halt. He opened his eyes and shook his head. It was daylight and they were in front of the stable at Castle Fraise. Chestnut had taken them home. One of the stable boys came out to meet them.

"How was your trip? You look sleepy."

"You wouldn't believe it," said James who stretched and yawned before Peggy and Billy crawled out of the carriage.

"We're here!" shouted Billy. "James, I don't know how you did it, but thank you! I feel like a new man."

"Nothing to it Billy, I did it with my eyes closed," smiled James.

"Good for you," he said while slapping James on the back. "You're a good friend, letting me sleep like that!"

"Come on, let's go inside," urged Peggy.

"We can't go inside dressed in these ridiculous outfits!" protested Billy.

"How else?" laughed Peggy.

"Well! Well! What have we here?" smiled the butler as he came out the back entrance that Billy and James had sneaked in through the day before.

Billy wanted to hide behind the bushes again until he was changed, but Colonel and Mrs. MacEve hurried out a few seconds later. They rushed toward Peggy and showered her with hugs and kisses.

"Welcome back to Castle Fraise, Hope. What a wonderful day this is." Mrs. MacEve cried, as did Peggy, and even the Colonel wiped his eyes.

"We're so sorry to learn of your misfortune. Miss Finney told us all about it," said the Colonel.

"Thank you Colonel. I'm doing fine now."

"So Miss Finney told us. And who are your friends?" chuckled the Colonel.

"James and Billy. They aren't dressed like their normal selves," laughed Peggy.

"Yes, we understand you had quite a time yesterday. The butler told us all about it."

"You don't know half of it. It was quite a night," sighed Billy.

"It's a pleasure to meet you Colonel and Mrs. MacEve," assured James, and Billy agreed.

"You must be starved. Come, have breakfast with us," Mrs. MacEve insisted. "We have so much news to catch up on."

"We are definitely starved, but would you mind if we changed before eating?" asked Billy.

"Not at all," said the Colonel with a hearty laugh. "We'll wait for you. Go along."

Billy especially was glad to be released from those ladies garments. In no time he and James washed up and changed. The butler led them to the dining room.

"Have a seat everyone," invited Mrs. MacEve.

"So, what brings you back so soon?" asked the Colonel with a mysterious smile that indicated he already knew.

"It's about this poem and my inheritance," stated Peggy, and she started to rattle off their adventures since arriving at the Castle, with Billy and James adding details. Colonel and Mrs. MacEve were in a state of shock.

"You have done extremely well. I believe your Papa would have been delighted with your accomplishment."

"Do you know how this dreamcatcher came to be here?" asked Peggy.

"I most certainly do," began the Colonel, "When your Mama and Papa discovered you were on the way, they were ecstatic. Shortly after they told us the good news, I was visiting Halifax, Nova Scotia, and stumbled upon a Mi'kmaq gentleman selling baskets and dreamcatchers. I thought the dreamcatcher would be something for you to remember us by."

"I met the gentleman. He's Sarah's Grandpa. We have become friends," informed Peggy, as she told them the whole story including the initials, O.K.

"Amazing!" commented the Colonel. "So what have you learned so far?"

"I'll tell you, but first I'd like your permission to find the answer to this next clue."

"By all means. I'll even accompany you as soon as we finish eating."

They all relished the delicious breakfast that was more like a feast. Although still a bit tired, Peggy was restless, waiting to start her search.

"I see you are anxious to begin," smiled the Colonel.

"Yes I sure am."

"We'll follow you, Peggy. I'm more than a little excited myself," said the Colonel.

Peggy marched directly to the kitchen, followed by the other four. She led the way into the secret passage.

"Wow! Isn't this great?" exclaimed Billy. "How'd you know about this?"

"Miss Finney showed me. Now, let's see, the three steps must be either at the beginning or end of the stairs," reasoned Peggy.

She searched for evidence at the base of the third step. "Nothing," she said.

"I knew it," muttered Billy. "Didn't I tell you?"

"Never mind. Let's go to the third step from the top," suggested Peggy.

"Doesn't look any different from the other steps," said Billy in a disappointed tone.

Peggy paid no attention and yanked on every stone on the third step. Nothing.

"See, I told you," scoffed Billy.

"Just wait a minute, you pessimist," insisted Peggy as she felt along the riser. A large stone in the left corner made a jiggling sound. "It's loose!" shouted Peggy.

Billy lowered the lamp, eager to see if this was another disappointment.

"It's stuck."

"Look out, I'll yank it out," insisted Billy.

"No you won't, just be patient. It's coming," said Peggy, as the stone slipped out.

"Who would have guessed it?" exclaimed Billy. The stone had been so well positioned; nobody would suspect it hadn't been cemented in place. Behind it was a small cavity.

"Would you look at that? Sneaky, eh? Can't be much treasure in there, though. Reach in, Peggy," encouraged Billy, growing more impatient by the second.

"I feel a small, wooden box," she said, as her heart began to race. "I wonder what's inside." She sat on the step, placing the box on her lap.

"Open it," demanded Billy. "What are you waiting for?"

"There's a hole in the back corner," she said and stuck her finger through it, but abruptly let out a terrified scream.

"What's wrong?" shouted James.

Peggy yanked her finger out of the hole and before she

could answer, a mouse jumped out, and raced down the steps.

"A mouse," laughed Billy. "You're scared of a silly little mouse?"

"It bit my finger. You would have hollered too," insisted Peggy. "Lucky it didn't break my skin. I might have caught rabies."

"Well since it didn't, open the box," said James.

Billy held the lamp so all could see. Cautiously, she slid back the latch and lifted the lid. The box was divided into two sections. A neat pile of paper formed a cozy mouse nest in one side and a number of gold coins in the other.

"Gold!" exclaimed Billy. "Look at the gold coins."

Peggy studied some of the coins and then picked up the small corner of paper that wasn't chewed. The only word legible was, DREAMCATCHER, in capital letters.

"I love being right, but this is one time I wish I wasn't," sighed Billy.

"There's another piece of paper folded under these coins," said Peggy.

"What's on it? I hope the mouse didn't chew that up too," said Billy.

"Only the corner. I think the rest is alright," said Peggy hopefully.

An unexpected voice echoed through the passage, startling everyone, "Why is Hope, I mean Peggy screaming? What's going on?"

"A mouse bit Peggy's finger, but everything's fine, Miss Finney," assured Colonel MacEve. "Peggy has found something that belongs to her; it's from her Papa."

"Well for land's sake, a mouse? What did you find, anyway?" she asked as she approached.

"We're about to find out," said Billy.

The suspense grew as each one watched. Billy was the most impatient.

"Come on, what's taking you so long, Peggy?"

"I don't want to tear it."

"I know that, but this is getting ridiculous. Hurry up!"

Peggy began unfolding the paper. A detailed map showed an island in a bay where a treasure was buried. Everything was marked with exact precision. In the center of the map were the words, 'The secret to get past the water tunnels is....' Since the map was folded twice and the mouse had chewed one corner, it left a hole where the message had been written. The only other words below the hole were, 'nly time will tell.' Peggy just sat quietly holding the map close to her heart. She held the dreamcatcher in the other hand and gently rubbed it between her nose and lip. Feathers brushed against her face.

"What did Papa write?" she questioned, deep in thought. "Is this the way it's going to end?"

Billy spoke again.

"Oh it's just as well, anyway. Can you imagine what Peggy would be like if she were filthy rich? We wouldn't be good enough for her. She'd leave the Cove for sure and buy one of those fancy houses in Halifax. She'd become a rich society woman. Nay, I think it's better if she stays just like she is."

"Billy!" said Peggy in shock. "Do you realize what you're saying? Since when did you care about me or what I did?"

"Yeah Billy, are you mellowing in your old age?" teased James.

For the first time in his life since knowing Peggy, Billy was dumbfounded. With all eyes glued on him, he stood there stuttering, trying desperately to find a word to save face. He felt heat rising to his head and knew his ears were turning red with embarrassment. Peggy was the most surprised of all. James came to his rescue.

"Oh, he's just trying to make you feel good, Peggy. He didn't know what else to say. Isn't that right, Billy?"

"Yeah, James, of course."

"By the way, Billy, if I ever become rich I'm going to do exactly as you said, except for one thing," smiled Peggy.

"What's that?"

"I plan to hire you as my servant. You'll have to do whatever my little heart desires without any backtalk. I'll be in my glory. What do you think of that?"

"Over my dead body! That'll be the day I ever serve you!" he laughed.

"Well, it's too bad I don't have the money to prove it."

"Yeah, I must agree, I was a little excited about you being rich. I just figured you'd buy me a big yacht or something to pay me back when I rescued you from that tower of death. Anyway, that's not going to happen so you'll just have to put up with me."

"There's no point crying over spilled milk. I did find my family. Right, Colonel?"

"Yes, you did. But I think you may have discovered more treasure than you realize."

"What do you mean by that?"

"You'll understand someday. Valuable treasure isn't always money, you know. So now what, Hope; or should we call you Peggy?"

"Peggy is what I like best."

"Very well, Peggy it is. Is there anything we can do for you?"

"I've been thinking, would you mind if I stayed with you for the night? We could leave tomorrow, but I want to spend time with you and Mrs. MacEve. I have a lot of questions."

"We would be delighted to have you," said Mrs. MacEve. You may sleep in the guest room where your folks always stayed whenever they came to visit."

"James, would you mind?" asked Peggy.

"No. It's not a problem with me, but if you don't mind Colonel, I'd like to return to the *Senora*. We need to get supplies and let Winkle know we're fine."

"For sure, my man, but we'll supply you with flour, potatoes, carrots, and smoked meat. I'll have Miss Finney provide plenty of bread and cookies as well. But first I'm sure you'd like to have a proper tour of the castle."

"Yes sir!" they all agreed as the Colonel led the way. After they finished their tour, Mrs. MacEve led Peggy and the others to the guest room.

"This is where you'll be sleeping Peggy. I hope you like it."

"It's beautiful," she said, and stood absorbing its beauty with joy and sorrow. It was the strangest feeling, knowing she had been here before, but not having any recollection. The thing that puzzled her most was the model of a ship with the name that sent chills down her spine. To make sure she wasn't seeing things, she moved closer. There was no mistake. In fine letters was the name; DREAMCATCHER. Her heart almost stopped.

Mrs. MacEve gave the history of the room and the entire list of important guests who stayed there. Billy was impressed to say the least. James and Colonel MacEve watched Peggy, who was absorbed with the model ship. When Mrs. MacEve finished, the room was silent.

"Thank you Mrs. MacEve, this has been great. I think we should be moving on, don't you Billy?"

"I was enjoying Mrs. MacEve's history lesson. Better than any I've ever had in school."

"I'm sure Winkle is at his wit's end by now, wondering how we are doing. We really should be off," insisted James.

"Colonel, could we stay here for a few minutes? I'd like to talk to you alone," asked Peggy.

"Not at all. Mrs. MacEve will take James and Billy to the butler. He'll make sure they get plenty of provisions. We'll be along before you leave, James."

"Sure thing," said James, as he, Mrs. MacEve, and Billy left.

Alone with the Colonel, Peggy rubbed her hand along the model ship. "Do the hatches open?"

"Why don't you see for yourself," replied the Colonel.

Peggy lifted one hatch and looked in. It was empty. Then she opened the second. It too was empty. The Colonel watched without saying a word.

"Colonel, I thought there was a connection between this model and that chewed piece of paper in the box. The only word left on it was DREAMCATCHER. When I saw this model, I was sure there was another clue inside."

"That's a clever observation," agreed the Colonel.

As Peggy covered the hatch, disappointment was written on her face. Not wanting to give up, she studied every part of the vessel for a clue. She recited the poem in her mind while searching. She remembered the last line, 'Only time will tell'. A key hung from the anchor of the model ship. It looked almost exactly like the one used to wind the clock at Janet's. The wheels in her mind began turning. She held the key with interest, and remembered what she had seen in the library on their tour.

"Let's go to the library, Colonel," she said excitedly.

"Most certainly," he agreed, beaming like a lighthouse on a stormy night as they made their way.

As they entered library, Peggy replied, "I think I have it."

"Have what, my dear?"

"Does this clock have anything to do with my inheritance?" she asked.

"You are as sharp as a two-edged sword. Why do you ask?"

"Papa loved riddles; the entire poem has clues to the treasure's location. A dreamcatcher is a ridiculous place to disclose the location of my inheritance; anyone could have taken it. I'm sure Papa wouldn't have been that careless, if he was as wise as you say. It looks like the last words on this map could be *'Only time will tell.'* May I open the clock door?"

"Yes, you may," he agreed, beaming even more as his chest seemed to grow a few inches wider.

Peggy slowly opened the clock door. She nervously tried the key. It fit perfectly.

"There is more to my inheritance, isn't there?"

"Not any more," smiled Colonel MacEve.

"What do you mean?" asked Peggy, puzzled by his answer.

"There is no doubt about it! You are your Papa's daughter. You have surpassed my greatest expectations. I argued, telling him how utterly ridiculous his idea was, but to no avail. He wanted to be certain you were wise and sharp too. I told him you would never be able to solve the mystery. I can tell you I am overjoyed to admit I was wrong. Placing the key to wind the clock is the end of your search. If you had not been able to solve the mystery, I was to wait until you were twenty and five years of age before telling you about your inheritance. Now, you are to receive the total sum of your Papa's wealth."

Peggy fell back into a chair, speechless, staring in utter amazement.

"Now you have solved the riddle, know who you are, and where you're from, but still can't remember your past. Was it worth it all?"

"Yes, a thousand times, yes!"

"Wonderful. Now you may get on with your life. Do you wish to remain in Scotland, here at the castle? I am your legal guardian. However, knowing your situation in Nova Scotia, I won't insist you stay. Miss Finney told us about the joy you brought back to Mary and her family since their loss of Elizabeth. What is your wish?"

"I'm happy to know you are my guardian and that you are letting me choose where I want to live. My family and closest friends are in Nova Scotia. I'd like to live with them, but I really want to come back for a longer stay."

"We'd be delighted! You're always welcome at Castle Fraise. You're family, remember?"

"I shall never forget," assured Peggy, slowly looking down.

"Is something troubling you?" asked the Colonel.

"What is my inheritance worth? A little, or a lot?"

"I'd say you are a very wealthy lady," confirmed the Colonel.

"Phew!" gasped Peggy, still in a state of shock and remained silent.

"What's on your mind?" asked the Colonel as he held Peggy's hand.

"Do you think I should tell anyone about my inheritance?"

"That's entirely up to you. How do you feel about it?"

"I'm dumbfounded, but I'll be able to make Billy my servant. Won't he be in for a surprise?"

"No doubt."

"But I'm saddened too. I'd give all my money away to have Mama and Papa back. Just knowing they spent time here, and Papa held this key... well it's pretty sad," she admitted.

"I understand. If there is anything I can do..."

"I know. You've been so helpful and patient. Thank you."

"Patient! If you only knew, it was a painful task keeping quiet and not giving any hints, but I gave my word not to help. You were to be on your own as far as figuring out the riddle."

"It all makes sense now. You had such funny looks on your face at times."

"There were tense moments, I wondered if you would solve the riddle. But what makes me angry is the danger you were in with the Knottys and Mr. Betts. I can't believe what you've been through."

"I'm thankful to be alive after dealing with them, that's for sure. I'm glad that's over!"

"So what is your decision? Will you keep it a secret or not?"

"I think I'll keep it a secret, just between the two of us."

"Mrs. MacEve knows about your inheritance, but she will not breathe a word, I can assure you."

"Then it's settled. A secret it is."

After Peggy and the Colonel finished their little talk, they headed for the stable where James and Billy were preparing to leave.

"I'll have one of he stable boys go along with you to bring back the wagon," said the Colonel.

"Thank you very much Colonel," said James.

"You are most welcome. It's been our pleasure. We'll see you tomorrow," he assured them as James, Billy, and the stable boy left.

Peggy spent time with the Colonel, who gave her wise advice on how to manage her inheritance.

"You have a tidy sum in those gold coins, but I'll give you more than enough to see you through until your inheritance arrives at a Bank of Nova Scotia, in Halifax. I won't send it all at once, but in three or four shipments. That way if anything unfortunate happens, you won't lose all your money. You may wish to leave a portion of you inheritance here in Scotland."

"I don't mind," agreed Peggy.

"You'll have to keep your correspondence and account information private if you don't want anyone to know your business. I'm sure you are capable of that. I'll still be overseeing your financial matters until you're eighteen. That was you Papa's wish."

"That's fine by me."

"Good, then I think we're finished."

Peggy spent the remainder of the day with Mrs. MacEve and Miss Finney. By bedtime, she was worn out. Stifling a yawn, she sighed, "I'm exhausted."

"Come along," offered Mrs. MacEve, accompanying Peggy up the stairs to the guest room. To Peggy's surprise, everything was laid out in neat array. Water in the basin, face cloth and towels, and a flannel night gown just her size. She didn't know that Mrs. MacEve had asked Miss Finney to dab a little perfume on the pillows. Peggy's Mama left a little bottle of it in the guest room.

"I have a few things to do while you're getting ready for bed. I'll be back shortly," assured Mrs. MacEve.

Peggy stood for a number of minutes absorbing every detail of her surroundings that she hadn't noticed earlier while focusing on the model ship.

A large four-posted bed was covered with a fancy, gold fringe around the top; and was skirted at the bottom. The soft, inviting bed reminded Peggy of sleeping in the clouds. A washstand stood in the corner and a comfortable chair was placed at the foot of the bed. Family pictures decorated the walls, while a beautiful rug covered the stone floor. As the room was located on the fourth floor, the view overlooking the gardens would be splendid when the sun rose in the morning.

Realizing Mrs. MacEve would soon return, Peggy quickly prepared for what she hoped would be a well-deserved sleep. She was about to brush her hair when Mrs. MacEve walked in.

"Here, let me, if you don't mind."

"No, not all," smiled Peggy. She had missed Mary's combing since leaving the Cove.

"I know you told Colonel MacEve you wanted to live with Mary and her family, but if you ever change your mind, don't hesitate to come live with us."

"I've thought about living here, but for now my mind is made up, I do want to go back. You don't have to wonder if I'll be sorry after we leave."

"That was my concern, but you seem to be sure of your decision, just like your Papa," smiled Mrs. MacEve as she continued brushing until Peggy's eyes began to close.

"I'm falling asleep."

"Slide in," said Mrs. MacEve as she turned back the covers. "Good night and sleep well."

"Thank you. I don't think that'll be a problem. I'm beat," yawned Peggy as Mrs. MacEve tucked her in.

Peggy reached for the picture of her, her Mama, and Papa before gently placing her lips to it. Her head sank into the fluffy pillow, which she hugged dearly. The fragrance on the pillow brought a smile to her lips. She remembered it was her Mama's perfume. As she drifted off, she felt a gentle kiss on her forehead, "Sleep well, my dear child. We love you," whispered Mrs. MacEve.

Peggy slept soundly.

Chapter 11
Chased by Pirates

At the crack of dawn, Peggy woke, excited to begin her long journey home, but the excitement quickly turned to a struggle. Out of the blue, thoughts of staying in Scotland, the comforts at Castle Fraise, and being with relatives became rather appealing. With her wealth, there was no limit to what she could do. Her thoughts ran wild, as she compared the simple life at the Cove to the luxuries of the castle. But picturing Mary's disappointment and grief after James presented the wrenching news that she wouldn't be living with them any more quickly erased all such foolish notions, and she prepared for the day. Racing to the kitchen, she was greeted by Miss Finney.

"Well, aren't you up bright and early?"

"Yes, and I'm starved."

"Come to the dinning room. Mrs. MacEve and the Colonel insist you have a hearty breakfast with all the trimmings and finest cutlery. They're waiting."

After a pleasant breakfast, the Colonel and Mrs. MacEve drove Peggy to the *Senora*. Peggy savored every minute.

Peggy wasn't the only one savoring the scenes that morning. Mr. Betts was giving Mr. and Mrs. Knotty a tour of his operations. It was down to business immediately. A shipment had arrived and needed clearing from the customs office. This would be Mr. Knotty's first assignment. He remembered his last trip there and how he sidestepped Mr. Betts when he purchased the tickets to Nova Scotia. There would be no sidestepping again. Oliver dreaded his working conditions already. The future looked very grim.

At the *Senora*, Peggy, the Colonel, and Mrs. MacEve were surprised with all the hustle and bustle. Winkle had put his clever talents to good use while James and Billy had been on their adventure of rescuing Peggy. Winkle had posted a sign high on the rigging that read, 'WANTED, FREIGHT TO NOVA SCOTIA.' A merchant was pleased to strike a deal with a large shipment of wool that was destined for Halifax. The cargo put James' mind at ease because he would now be able to help pay Captain Simms for 'borrowing' the *Senora*.

As Peggy jumped from the carriage, and before she had a chance to stop him, Billy reached for her suitcase, which was actually Rosa's.

"What's in that, gold?" he asked jokingly after feeling how heavy it was.

"Of course, Billy. Now I can hire you to be my servant."

"With your luck, you're never going to see that day," he laughed.

Colonel and Mrs. MacEve were astonished at Peggy's answer to Billy, but saw how clever she was in telling the truth. He didn't believe a word she said.

The MacEves gave their bittersweet farewells to Peggy and her companions, and left. Peggy went to the stern of the *Senora* where she could watch until the Colonel and Mrs. MacEve were out of sight. They waved to each other as the carriage rounded the corner. It was an emotional moment for all, but especially Peggy.

Things had definitely improved since their escape from Mr. Betts. Soon they would be on their way home. Peggy couldn't wait, but her excitement turned to horror the instant she saw two of Mr. Betts' men, Grub and Cage, strutting along the dock. Her stomach churned at the sight of them. She hoped they would walk on by without noticing James or Billy. She stepped behind the mast and watched. Grub and Cage approached the merchant who owned the shipment of wool that was being loaded into the *Senora*.

Peggy ran on the port side of the *Senora* to avoid being seen by the goons. She called to James and Billy in a loud whisper, but they were so busy talking and laughing while loading the wool, they didn't hear her. She grabbed a long gaff and hooked Billy by the seat of his pants.

"What's going on here?" demanded Billy as he turned and saw Peggy waving them over.

"Two of Betts' goons are arguing with that merchant," gasped Peggy.

Billy and James turned to look. By now, Winkle stood beside the merchant.

"Is there a problem?"

"Apparently so," said the merchant, "but I'm not convinced. These two gentlemen claim Mr. Betts is entitled to a tariff for loading freight. They're demanding payment immediately."

"That's ridiculous, just a minute. I'll be right back," said Winkle, who headed to board the *Senora* to talk with James and Billy.

Cage and Grub searched the deck of the *Senora*. They spotted Billy and James. Then they looked at each other. Grub took Cage by the arm and pushed him aside.

"Those'r the two clowns who escaped the night befur last. D'ya see that girl?"

Cage moved from side to side to get a better look. For a split second, he saw Peggy.

"Yes sir," said Cage. "That's gotta be her. She's tryin' to hide."

"Quick! Tell the boss. He's at the customs office doin' legal work with Mr. Knotty."

Cage instantly marched off.

Winkle knew the two men were Mr. Betts' goons and that they were after Peggy. James and Billy told him the full story the day before. Within seconds, James, Winkle, and Billy made the decision to leave immediately. Winkle and Billy rushed to hoist the sails while James went to inform the merchant. As he approached, Grub moved a short distance away, pretending not to recognize James.

"I'm sorry sir, but we must leave instantly. Those two men are ruthless and we have a serious situation. We'll deliver the wool that's on board, but you'll have to find another ship for the rest."

"But you can't take only a portion of my shipment," protested the merchant.

"We don't have a choice. I'm sorry. By the way, have nothing to do with those men," said James, and he ran aboard the *Senora*.

All four untied the sails. To Peggy, it took forever. She and Billy hoisted the jibs while James and Winkle raised the mainsail. "We'll leave the foresail until we're under way," shouted James.

Finally they were set to leave. Billy and James untied the *Senora* and with the aid of some men along the dock, they pushed off. The gentle breeze caught the jibs and slowly pulled the *Senora* around.

The instant Grub saw James giving the orders to leave, he left.

While they were preparing to leave, Peggy kept looking for Mr. Betts or his men to return. They were relieved to be under way before they arrived. James and Billy raised the foresail as Winkle navigated the *Senora* towards the entrance of the harbour, where not too far off shore, laid a blanket of thick fog. Everyone breathed easier.

To brighten her spirits and forget about Mr. Betts and his goons, Peggy watched the seagulls. The one circling overhead reminded her of Hector. She reached for the telescope to get a bird's eye view. As the gull swooped low to snatch a scrap of food from the water, a flash through the scope caught Peggy's attention. A lady wearing an outlandish hat caused her stomach to churn. Instantly she forgot about the seagull and focused on three people climbing aboard an old ship that was anchored closer to the harbour entrance. It looked more like a pirate ship than a cargo vessel. There was no mistaking their identity.

"Mrs. Knotty, Mr. Knotty, and Mr. Betts," gasped Peggy. "Won't they ever give up?"

"James! Come quick! Look!" she shouted.

James grabbed the telescope and shook his head. "Winkle and Billy, come here."

"What's up James? You look worried," asked Winkle.

"Take a look," he said, handing Winkle the telescope. "Over there, on that ship."

"I think we've got company," said Winkle.

"Let me see," said Billy, grabbing the scope. "Betts and the Knottys."

Peggy watched the ship, which the Knottys boarded. The cannon at the bow and another at the stern, made her quake. The crew, a rough looking bunch, were grimy and greasy. The captain was almost as scruffy as the crew. He was a burly man with a large belly and a scraggly, dark beard. "Do you think they're pirates, James?" asked Peggy.

"Could be."

"What are we going to do?" she asked fearfully.

"We'll outsmart them," assured James.

Peggy looked through the telescope again. To her disgust, Mr. Betts aimed his telescope, staring her right in the eye.

"That Mr. Betts is looking right at me."

Then she noticed something else.

"They're raising the sails!" she shouted to James.

"What's your plan there, James old boy?" asked Winkle.

"We have to slow them down so we can disappear. This is one time I'm thankful for that fogbank," said James.

"They're pulling the anchor!" yelled Peggy. "Can't you go faster, James?"

"We're trying."

A steady breeze pushed the *Senora* toward freedom. Winkle manned the helm while James and Billy set every inch of sail. Winkle talked to the *Senora* as if she understood his words.

"Come on, girl, show them what you're made of," he coaxed.

"Aim straight for them Winkle."

"Don't we want to get away from them?" shouted Peggy terrified. "They're getting too close!"

"You know what to do Winkle," said James seriously.

"Yes sir, James," said Winkle, and he sailed on.

"We're going to crash," yelled Peggy.

The crew, Mr. Knotty, and Mr. Betts were shouting and waving their hands frantically.

"You idiots, you're going to ram us."

"Hold her Winkle, don't change course."

Peggy and Billy ran to the stern of the *Senora*, ready to jump overboard.

Mr. Knotty yelled, "There's no need to be afraid, we just want to talk to Peggy."

"There's nothing to talk about," replied James.

"Stop this minute or I'll have you blown out of the water," shouted Mr. Betts, whose face was now red with anger.

The Captain was shaking his fist at Winkle as he continued on the collision course. At the last second, the Captain of the *Pursuit* shouted the order: "Hard to port! Come about!"

"Keep onto them Winkle. Don't let up yet," ordered James.

"I'm with you!" he shouted back.

The *Pursuit* was forced to come about and head back in the opposite direction. The crew raced around the ship like their pants were on fire. The ship lost speed. The crew rushed to adjust the sails, hoping to gain enough speed to come about again before the *Senora* vanished into the fog.

"Good work Winkle," congratulated James.

"Good work!" shouted Peggy. "I could see the whites in the Knottys' and Mr. Betts' eyes."

"I saw it in the Captain's and crew," shouted Billy. "I thought you were insane, James."

"They had to stay clear of us. We had the right of way," smiled James as the *Senora* disappeared into the fog.

"Winkle, they aren't far behind, point the *Senora* so she's in irons!" ordered James quietly. Obediently, the *Senora*'s bow headed directly into the wind, while she sat quietly and at a standstill. Every soul remained silent, listening and watching. The *Pursuit* was closer than expected and the sound of the waves splashing against her hull gave Peggy the shivers. A voice called out.

"They can't be far from here. Five pounds to the man who spots her!"

"There they are!" shouted Mrs. Knotty.

"Turn hard to starboard!" ordered the captain. "Get ready to fire."

Peggy whispered, "Fire? They're going to shoot at us. Do something!"

"Winkle, bring her around, let's get out of here," signaled James, but a fiery ball of orange flashed through the fog followed by a thundering boom.

"Duck everyone!" shouted James. All four hit the deck as a cannon ball ripped through the foremost jib.

"Hurry Billy, help me set the sails. Winkle, give her a beam reach until we pick up speed and change to close hauled. That'll make the *Senora* a harder target. They'll be guessing where we are by the time they reload that cannon and position for another shot. No more talking anyone," whispered James.

"Come here everyone," motioned Peggy. "I have an idea. Let's lower a lifeboat, let it out with a long rope, and make a noise. Then pull the boat in real quick. They'll think we're a long way back, and be aiming in the wrong direction."

"That's a good idea!" said Billy. "Why didn't I think of that one too? Come on fellows, help me get that boat ready before they fire again," whispered Billy.

"Actually I was thinking I should go," said Peggy.

"You're not going anywhere! It's too dangerous," insisted Billy.

"Well I have news for you. I'm lighter than you, and you're stronger than I am, so the three of you can pull me in faster. We don't have time to argue. Get that boat in the water," she whispered.

"I don't like it any more than you Billy," said James, "but she's right. Let's hurry."

In no time, James and Billy had the boat in the water and Peggy was drifting far from the *Senora*. She trembled at the thought of being blown to bits by a cannonball. I suppose I won't feel it if it hits me, she thought. Finally the rope came taut. She smacked the oar on the water and let out a deafening scream.

Winkle had tied the wheel to keep the *Senora* on course.

"Pull you guys," signaled James as they rushed to bring Peggy back. About a third of the way in, another deafening explosion blasted from the *Pursuit*. Peggy hit the bottom of the boat as a cannonball whizzed overhead. A huge splash some distance away indicated that Peggy's idea worked. Peggy was soon pulled on board.

"Congratulations, Peggy," whispered Billy.

"Thank you," she smiled.

"They were firing high, aiming for the mast. Lucky for us, eh?" whispered Billy.

"You mean lucky for me," sighed Peggy. "I think I'll keep any more ideas to myself from now on."

"They've passed. Turn the *Senora* south and let her run, Winkle. I think we outmaneuvered them," whispered James.

"James, you had me worried," said Billy. "But I feel a lot better now."

Aboard the *Pursuit*, Mr. Betts was pacing the deck.

"You told me you were the best, now you've lost them again," snarled Mr. Betts to the captain.

"I can't help it if the *Senora* points better than my ship. There's no use in arguing. Keep your eyes peeled everyone. We'll find them," assured the captain.

"You better," warned Mr. Betts.

Within a half hour, things were looking brighter. Too bright, as a matter of fact. The sun burnt off the fog before the *Senora* was out of sight. One thing James knew for sure, the Knottys would surely see them.

"They are coming after us," he warned after looking through the telescope.

"What are we going to do?" asked Peggy.

"Right now we don't have much choice but to outrun them. If they are gaining on us, it's not by much."

By late evening, the *Pursuit* was too close for comfort. Tension had mounted.

"Winkle, let me take the wheel; you and Billy light the navigation lamps. When it's good and dark, we'll blow them out, and sail west until we're sure the Knottys have gone past."

"Look James, the fog is coming back," said Peggy.

"I know."

"This is another time I'm happy to see that fog," smiled Winkle. "I think God is on our side."

"Mary would say 'Amen!' to that," replied Peggy.

"You're right again," agreed Billy.

"Let's head slightly east, first. Maybe that'll fool them," reasoned James.

As the night drew on, and the fog thickened, it gave the *Senora* a hiding place. Winkle was becoming impatient.

"I'd say it's time to come about, James."

"Fine, blow out the lights. Get ready, everyone. Here we go!" The *Senora* headed west. Shortly, voices could be heard from the passing vessel.

"You outsmarted them again, James," congratulated Winkle.

"I'm getting tired of this cat and mouse game. I hope that's the last we see of them," sighed Peggy.

They sailed on for a while longer, until James figured it was time to change course.

"Let's get ready to come about, you guys."

"I see a glow; that must be Bell Rock Lighthouse. Come on, James, we're getting mighty close," warned Winkle.

"We're coming about everyone," ordered James.

Peggy faced James just as he turned the wheel. With a terrifying scream Peggy yelled, "Stop James! Look out!"

James stared in horror. The *Pursuit*, aiming straight toward them on the starboard, prevented the *Senora* from coming about. They were being forced onto Bell Rock. A loud explosion scared the daylights out of them. There was an awful whoop, as the jib caught a cannon ball, ripping a hole through it.

Bell Rock Lighthouse

"Duck, everyone. We'll jibe!" yelled James in a panic.

The *Senora* swung toward Bell Rock with sails whipping around. There was a terrible crash. All but James headed for cover, expecting the masts to come crashing down. The *Senora* listed hard, almost dumping Winkle and Billy into the dark sea. Peggy held onto the gunnels for dear life.

"James! Swing her into the wind!" yelled Winkle.

The *Senora* slowly righted herself.

"Away from the rock before we lose speed!" hollered Winkle .

"I am!" he shouted, and spun the wheel frantically. The *Senora* steadied as Winkle and Billy rushed to pull on the yards and set the sails. Bell Rock was dangerously close. Swirling foam licked at the waterline and jagged rocks brushed past while breaking waves roared over Bell Rock.

With the hustle and bustle, nobody paid attention to the problems threatening the *Pursuit.* She too swung to clear Bell Rock. The terrible crash wasn't the *Senora's* masts, but the *Pursuit's* deadly blow. She heaved and groaned as she came to rest on Bell Rock.

As the *Senora* pulled away, Peggy shouted, "Listen! I thought I heard someone crying for help." She ran to the stern of the *Senora* looking and listening. All she could see was the faded outline of the *Pursuit*, disappearing from view.

"What did you hear?" asked Billy.

"Shh! There it is again."

Billy strained his ear.

"You're hearing things. It's the waves crashing against the rocks and the wind howling."

"Maybe you're right," doubted Peggy.

Her eyes searched, she saw nothing but the sea.

The *Senora* quickly sailed beyond Bell Rock, leaving behind the wave battered abutment, slick with seaweed and seafoam. Then, barely visible in the swirling water was a figure, and without warning, two hands suddenly burst from the water and grabbed onto the rocks.

Chapter 12
Homeward Bound

With the *Pursuit* out of commission, everyone on the *Senora* breathed easier as they sailed on, heading toward the Cove. It would take about a month to cross the Atlantic.

With weeks of fair weather, Peggy's mind began to ease. "Well, we'll soon be home," announced Winkle, who never seemed to have a care in the world.

"I can't wait," said Peggy. "Can you imagine what everyone will think when we get there?"

"Yeah! I wonder what Pa will do and how Rosa is making out. I hope she went to your place James, like I told her to."

"I'm sure Ma would make sure she is alright. I'm thinking about Captain Simms. What do you think he'll do to us, Winkle?"

"He's a pretty decent guy, but I'm sure he won't be too happy, especially if he lost most of his customers. I guess we'll just have to wait and see."

"I just hope we don't lose our jobs," said James. "I'll make it up to him somehow."

"Well, my family never knows when I'm coming or going, but this was the longest I've been away without contacting them. I'm sure word got back to them that we took off," reasoned Winkle. "One thing for sure, we'll all know soon."

With an estimated three days before arriving home, the red morning sky brought fear into Peggy's heart. Dark clouds gathered and brisk winds began churning the sea. James and Billy secured everything above and below deck.

"Looks like we're in for some stormy weather," Winkle observed. "Everything will be just fine Peggy," he assured her after seeing the worried look in her eyes.

She doubted that. As the day wore on, so did her fear. Foaming seas and sheets of rain battered the *Senora*. James and Billy reefed the sails, but the *Senora* still leaned at fearful angles. All through the night, Peggy didn't sleep. With the break of day and no worsening of the storm, she couldn't keep her eyes open any longer and slept until noon. By late afternoon the rain stopped and it appeared the winds had subsided. The three men seemed relieved and began to enjoy the action.

"Let's see how fast we can make the old girl go!" shouted Billy.

The wind had changed direction, providing the perfect angle to drive the *Senora* at top speed. She rose and dove through the swelling seas.

"I've never seen sail like this," yelled Winkle, beaming like he was master of the sea, while he was at the helm. "I wish Captain Simms could see her now!"

Peggy still wasn't convinced they really knew what they were doing. However, their excitement and laughter helped. The three were having so much fun; it was hard for her not to be caught up in the excitement. Each wanted a turn at the wheel, hoping to get the fastest speed. Then Billy yelled, "Peggy! Come take the wheel."

"Sure Billy, so you can make a fool of me again. No thanks."

"No, I'm serious. I'll hold it with you until you get the feel of it. And if I don't, James and Winkle can throw me overboard. Cross my heart and hope to die."

Peggy looked at James, who gave her the wink of approval.

"Alright. Just remember, there are sharks in these waters," she warned as she grabbed the wheel.

At first she was off course more than on, but after a while she began to get the hang of it. Billy even let go of the wheel and gave her full control. Exhilaration shot through her veins as she and the *Senora* bonded. Winkle threw a sou'wester on her head and saluted while James and Billy joined in. They were so focused on Peggy they paid no attention to the sea. Peggy let out a piercing squeal. A huge wave sent the *Senora* diving. Water washed over the gunnels, sweeping the three giddy sailors off their feet, and sending them sliding around the deck. Peggy was doing a bit of fancy footwork herself, slipping and sliding, but held onto the wheel for dear life. The *Senora* twisted and turned like a dizzy kid. By the time the three embarrassed sailors were back on their feet Peggy admitted, "That's enough for me. Here James, take over."

They took it in good humor, accusing Peggy of dunking them on purpose.

Shortly after, the three jolly sailors really became excited. Off to the port, appeared a set of sails.

"Would ya lookee there," shouted Billy. "Let's give them a run for their money."

Obviously, the captain of the other vessel was of the same mind. Both ships drew closer. Peggy's worries lightened with the potential of being rescued should those clowns sink the *Senora*. She became amused, listening to their plans to win the race, and watched with interest as they scurried about.

Pulling along side, the crews exchanged greetings and destinations. Another relief for Peggy came when the captain informed them he was heading to Lunenburg, Nova Scotia. That meant they would have company practically all the way home. She sighed. Things were looking up.

Then the cat and mouse game began. It was just like being with James and John and their fishing friends. First they had a run of small talk, and then subtly, they began their fancy maneuvers. Slowly, the *Senora* inched ahead. The opposing crew made no secret of their intent. The captain gave orders to raise all the sails, hoping to gain the lead. James followed suit.

It was a tight race, and if the *Gladys B* hadn't been laden with fish, she probably would have beaten them. Once satisfied they were the winners, James eased off, allowing the *Gladys B* to catch up. They sailed close at hand, day and night, until it was parting time.

Soon, they were only hours away from home. As the Cove coastline came into view, Peggy's heart began to race. Nothing could contain her excitement, especially when Hector showed up with his usual squealing and squawking. Everyone began singing and dancing around the deck, except for Winkle; he remained at the helm. It would be late afternoon when they'd drop anchor outside the Cove.

Every day since Peggy's disappearance, Rosa climbed the highest rocks, searching and hoping. Today the telescope focused on a schooner. She rubbed her eyes and

took a second look. Could it be? Her heart pounded for fear it wasn't true. Finally she was able to read the name 'Senora'. She ran for all she was worth. Her body was almost ahead of her feet as she raced through the Cove.

"They're coming! They're coming. The *Senora* is back," she shouted hysterically.

There was more commotion than the day Billy had toppled Susie's outhouse. By the time Billy and James dropped anchor, boats surrounded them, and bodies were crawling aboard in all directions. What a homecoming!

Mary was the first to climb on board, hugging and kissing Peggy, James, Billy, and Winkle. She could barely make out who was who through the tears that flowed so freely.

John and the boys, Peter and Joe, weren't as emotional, but their pleasure was far from hidden.

Rosa grabbed Billy and Peggy together and held on as though she was glued to them. Billy kept an eye open for his Pa. Rosa noticed his worried look.

"Billy, it's alright. Pa left a week after you and James went after Peggy."

It seemed the only ones from the Cove not on board the *Senora* were the folks too old to climb into a boat. Most of them lined the wharf, waiting for everyone to come ashore.

Questions flew in every direction. Finally, Peggy said, "Let's go home and have supper. Why don't we all meet in the hall at seven and we'll tell you all about our trip."

Everyone agreed and couldn't wait for the appointed time. What a night it was! Their adventures captivated every heart. At times the hall was filled with laughter, especially with the stories of Billy and James in their disguises. Others raised their eyebrows, shook their heads, and opened their mouths in shock. Even a few ladies shed the odd tear. Hours flew, as each told their story and answered questions. Congratulations were handed out to all four, for their bravery and determination; but Peggy was the real hero. It was well into the wee hours of the morning before everyone decided it was time to go home.

Before parting, James asked Billy if he would accompany him and Winkle in the morning while they returned the *Senora* to Captain Simms. He agreed, but Peggy overheard, and insisted on going as well. She secretly had some business to patch up with Captain Simms.

Anxiety kept James and Winkle from sleeping, so they had everyone awake and ready to sail at the first puff of wind. John hitched Jake to the wagon and headed to Captain Simms to bring them home.

Certain that his career was about to end, James became more fidgety the closer they came to French Village Harbour. Rounding MacDonald's Point, he stood at the bow to catch the first glimpse of the Simms' home. No doubt, Captain Simms was longing to know the whereabouts of his beloved ship.

James watched. A familiar figure was leaning back in a big wooden chair at the end of the wharf. It appeared he was resting. Suddenly he hopped to his feet as if he couldn't believe his eyes. He yelled the good news to his wife before jumping into a rowboat to meet his *Senora*. James was prepared for the worst as they tied up to the mooring and the Captain climbed aboard.

"For a minute I thought I was dreaming. Thank heavens you're all alive," he sighed. He ran his hands along the *Senora's* gunnels and held the wheel. "I was beginning to think you were all lost. I don't know if I should be mad or glad. What do you have to say for yourself?"

"Before you answer that, James, may I talk to you alone, Captain Simms?" asked Peggy. "It's important."

"Well, I guess so young lady. I'm curious to know what's so important. Come below."

Inside and away from all ears, Peggy began: "I have a confession to make, sir. It's my fault for all your heartache and worry."

"Nonsense," said Captain Simms. "Those Knottys should be strung up for kidnapping you. Why would you ever say such a thing?"

"Because...well...it's like this, sir," hesitated Peggy as she began her story.

Back on deck, Billy was the only one who didn't have anything to worry about, but when he heard a loud 'You what?!' explode from Captain Simms even he began to wonder what was going on. They couldn't hear any other words of the conversation.

"Thank you for being so patient and letting me explain; I hope you understand," said Peggy as she finished. Captain Simms looked into her eyes, dumbfounded and speechless.

"So you see, sir, I had no idea James would come after me. Please take this. It should be enough to cover your losses," and she handed him a number of gold coins.

Captain Simms, now even more bewildered and puzzled, rubbed his beard in deep thought.

"Please keep James and Winkle on. They were only trying to help me. By the way, you and I are the only two who know that I planned my own kidnapping. Do you think I need to tell anyone else?"

"Peggy! Peggy! You boggle my mind. Never have I met anyone quite like you. No, I don't think it's necessary to tell a soul. My lips are sealed. Now that I know the full story, I will not dismiss James or Winkle. They are fine sailors and it would be impossible to replace them. Let me think about your payment. I'll do the calculations and determine just how much your adventure cost. Fortunately, Joshua Dauphinee wasn't very busy. He delivered my freight with the Lorne so I didn't lose my customers. Now, let's go back on deck. No doubt James and Winkle are wondering if they still have a job."

"Thank you, Captain Simms. You are a kind and understanding man. I think you must be a lot like my Pa was," Peggy said as she shook his hand.

"You are welcome, young lady. Now let's give those two young men the good news."

"Aye, aye, sir!" replied Peggy with a sigh of relief, happy that she had done the right thing in telling Captain Simms the truth. "They must have ants in their pants by now."

They both laughed while climbing back on deck. James, Billy, and Winkle wondered what in the world those two had discussed when they saw the cheerful faces of Peggy and Captain Simms.

"Well, gentlemen, I think you deserve a rest after your horrific adventure. How about reporting back in two weeks?"

"Well sir, Winkle found a merchant who needed a shipment of wool taken to Halifax. We shouldn't wait that long," said James.

"Well done, Winkle, but I think you all need a rest. I'll have Joshua's crew help me. He's doing some repairs on the Lorne and they need the work. Now let's go ashore. I see John has arrived."

Stunned by his generosity and lack of hostility, James and Winkle nodded their heads in shock.

"Yes, sir. Thank you, sir!"

Back on shore, the adventurers piled onto the wagon and Captain Simms patted Peggy on the back and gave her a wink. She returned one, along with and an ear-to-ear smile.

As they drove away, Billy couldn't wait any longer. "What was all that winking about, and what did you say that made Captain Simms yell, 'you what?'"

"If I told you that, it wouldn't be a secret, would it?" she chuckled, looking into the sky mischievously, as if she knew something they didn't, and she did.

The End

Head of St. Margaret's Bay

Ingramport • • Boutilier's
                    Point

Blackpoint •

Queensland •

Hubbards •

Fox Point •

Mill Cove •

St. Margaret's
Bay

French Village Harbour •
Captain Simms
Uncle Willie's
Blacksmith Shop

• Tantallon

• Glen Haven

• French Village

MacDonald's Point

• Seabright

Sarah's Home
Wooden's River

Janet's Place
• Glen Margaret

• Hackett's Cove

Shut-in-Island •

Northwest Cove •

Aspotogan Peninsula •

• Indian Harbour

Peggy's Cove

Bayswater •

To West Dover

To Tancook Islands

Swiss Air 111 •
Crash Site

Special Thanks

A special "Thank you" to Kathleen MacDonald (Motion Pictures Inc.) who is my story editor, mentor and friend. She had her work cut out trying to keep me on course for over two and a half years. But after twelve drafts and a little polish she finally announced the glorious words, "It's finished."

A hearty, "Thank you," to every other soul who gave advice, encouragement and support. You are much appreciated. It would be nice to mention names, but some want to remain anonymous, and I'm sure I'd miss at least one wonderful person.

I'm thankful to God for the His many blessings and for the talent to write this book.

Through Peggy's story, I hope you will be challenged to do your best, never give up and learn valuable lessons that will help develop your character.

Please share your experiences if Peggy's story has been helpful to you.

Contact Ivan by mail or email at:

Ivan Fraser
C/O Peggy of the Cove
10235/6 Peggy's Cove Road
Glen Margaret NS Canada B3Z 3J1

ivan@peggyofthecove.com
www.peggyofthecove.com